AGATHA CHRISTIE

ENDLESS NIGHT

ADAPTED BY FRANÇOIS RIVIÈRE
ILLUSTRATED BY FRANK LECLERCQ

HARPER

Every Night and every Morn
Some to Misery are born.
Every Morn and every Night
Some are born to Sweet Delight,
Some are born to Sweet Delight,
Some are born to Endless Night.

William Blake
Auguries of Innocence

HARPER
An imprint of HarperCollins*Publishers*
77-85 Fulham Palace Road
Hammersmith, London W6 8JB
www.harpercollins.co.uk

First published by HARPER 2008
1

Comic book edition published in France as *La Nuit qui ne finit pas*
© Heupé SARL/Emmanuel Proust Éditions 2003
Based on *Endless Night* © 1967 by Agatha Christie Limited,
a Chorion Company. All rights reserved.
www.agathachristie.com

Adapted by François Rivière. Illustrated by Frank Leclercq.
English edition edited by David Brawn.

ISBN 978-0-00-727533-5

Printed and bound in China.

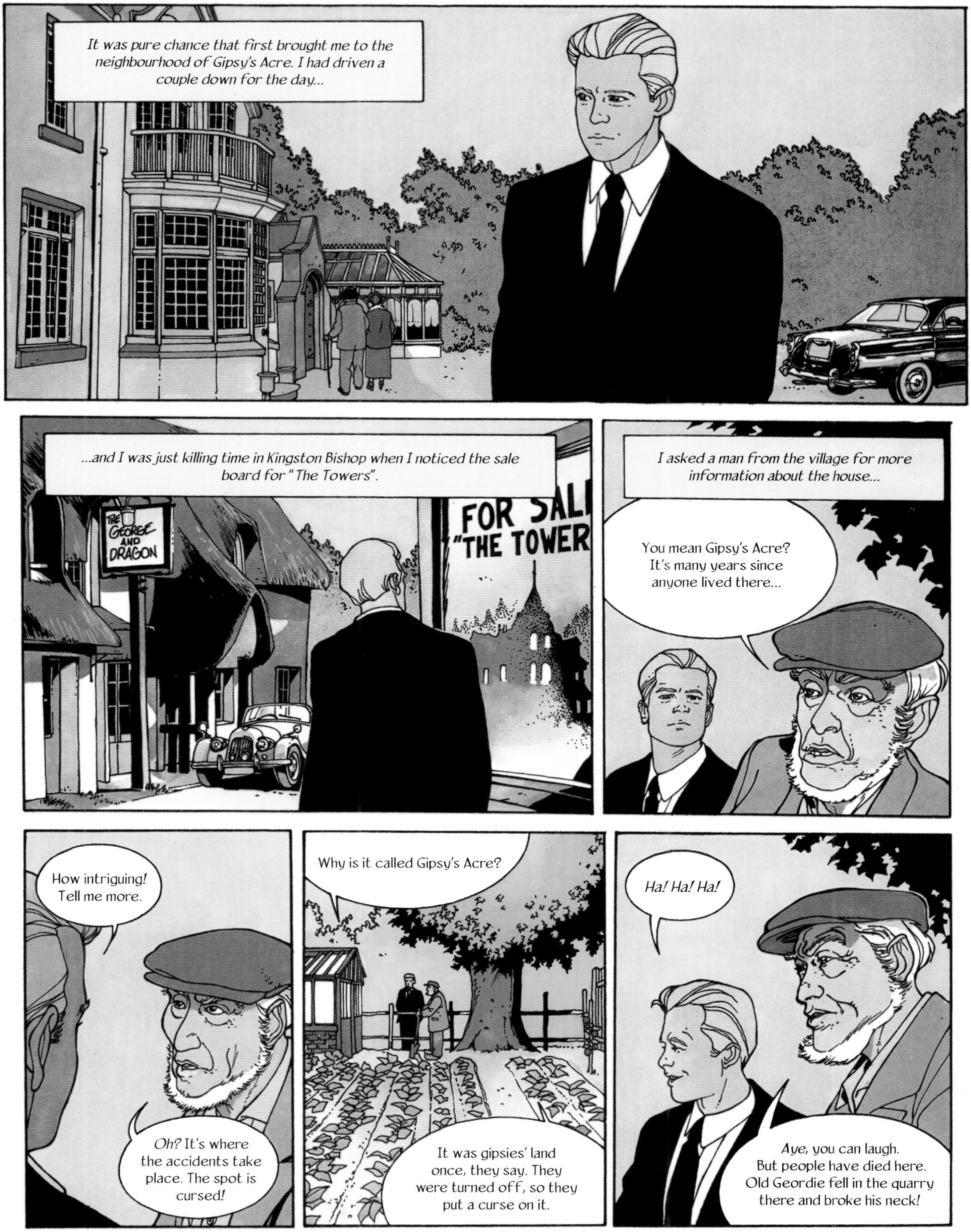
It was pure chance that first brought me to the neighbourhood of Gipsy's Acre. I had driven a couple down for the day...
...and I was just killing time in Kingston Bishop when I noticed the sale board for "The Towers".
THE GEORGE AND DRAGON
FOR SAL
"THE TOWER
I asked a man from the village for more information about the house...
You mean Gipsy's Acre? It's many years since anyone lived there...
How intriguing! Tell me more.
Oh? It's where the accidents take place. The spot is cursed!
Why is it called Gipsy's Acre?
It was gipsies' land once, they say. They were turned off, so they put a curse on it.
Ha! Ha! Ha!
Aye, you can laugh. But people have died here. Old Geordie fell in the quarry there and broke his neck!

I went up the road that wound up through the dark trees and came out at the top of the hill overlooking the sea. It was a marvellous view...

If you want gipsies, there's old Mrs Lee. She lives in the cottage at the end of the road.

And so...

Listen to me, young man. Forget Gipsy's Acre. Nothing good will come of it!

But it's up for sale. Do you know who is likely to buy it?

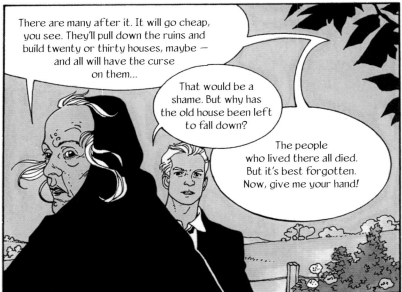

There are many after it. It will go cheap, you see. They'll pull down the ruins and build twenty or thirty houses, maybe — and all will have the curse on them...

That would be a shame. But why has the old house been left to fall down?

The people who lived there all died. But it's best forgotten. Now, give me your hand!

There's sorrow and danger for you here. Take my advice. Get out of Gipsy's Acre and don't come back!

And though I don't believe in fortune-telling, I had an uneasy feeling that the sinister old creature had just seen something in my palm...

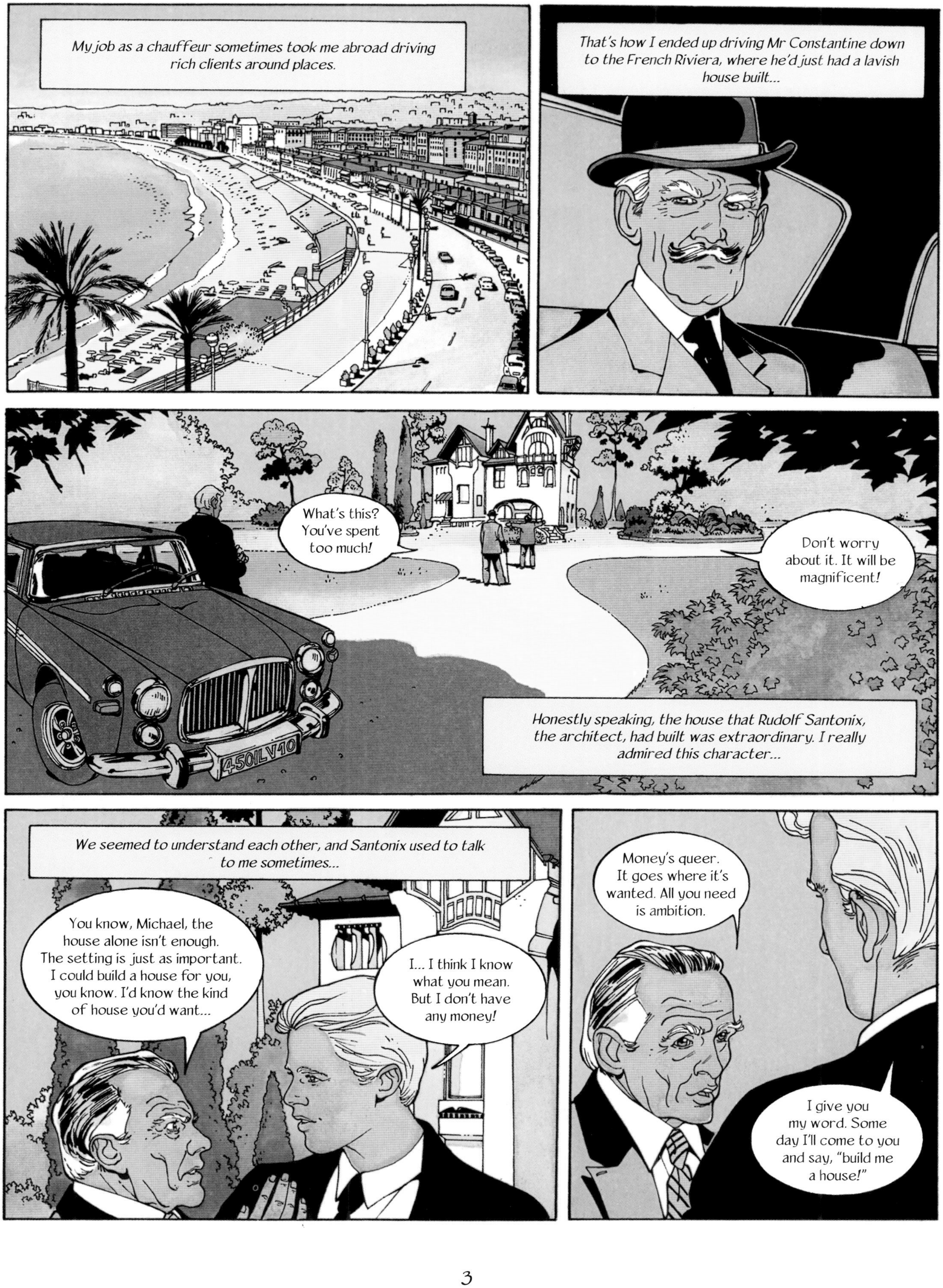
My job as a chauffeur sometimes took me abroad driving rich clients around places.
That's how I ended up driving Mr Constantine down to the French Riviera, where he'd just had a lavish house built...
What's this? You've spent too much!
Don't worry about it. It will be magnificent!
450ILV10
Honestly speaking, the house that Rudolf Santonix, the architect, had built was extraordinary. I really admired this character...
We seemed to understand each other, and Santonix used to talk to me sometimes...
You know, Michael, the house alone isn't enough. The setting is just as important. I could build a house for you, you know. I'd know the kind of house you'd want...
I... I think I know what you mean. But I don't have any money!
Money's queer. It goes where it's wanted. All you need is ambition.
I give you my word. Some day I'll come to you and say, "build me a house!"

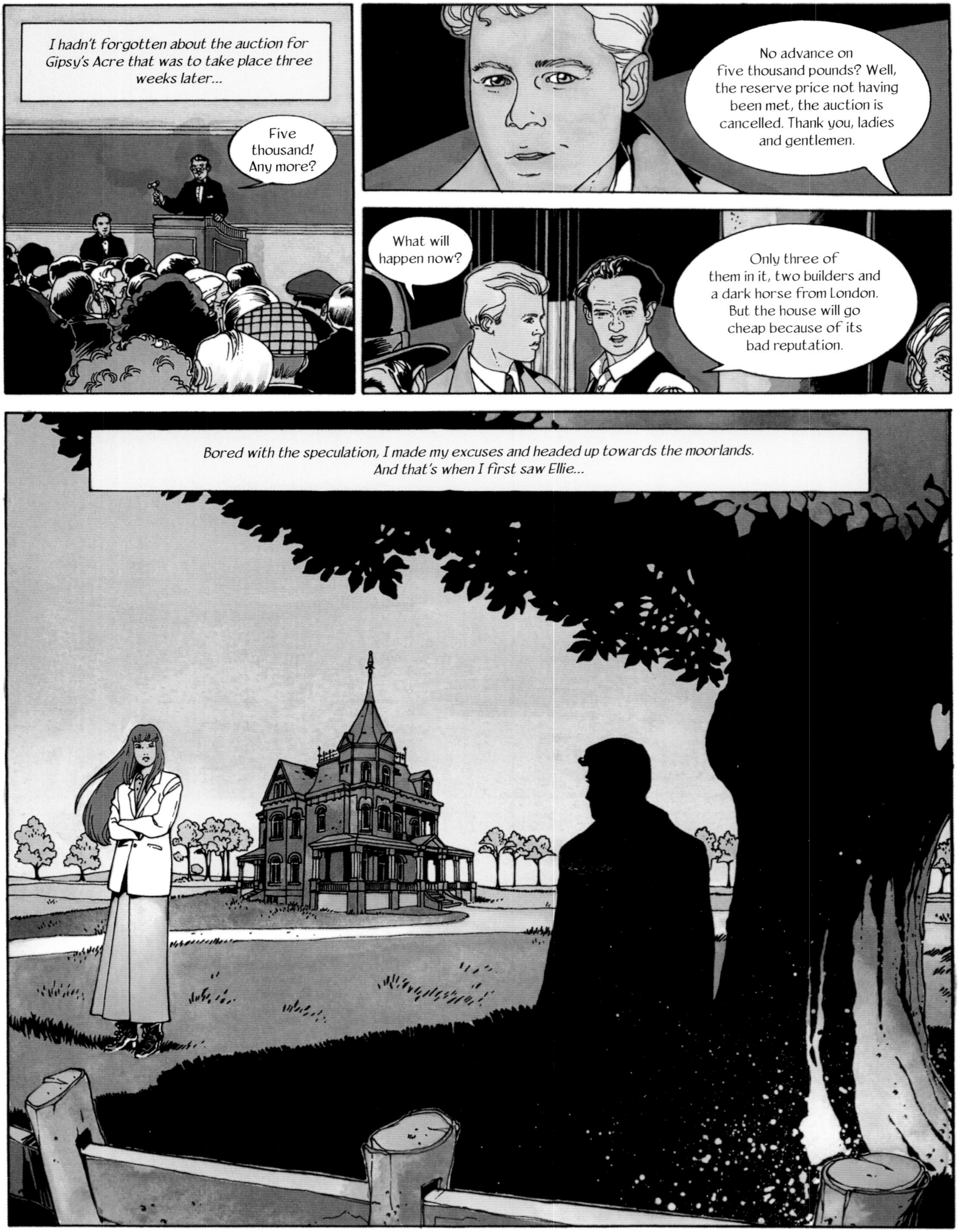
I hadn't forgotten about the auction for Gipsy's Acre that was to take place three weeks later...
Five thousand! Any more?
No advance on five thousand pounds? Well, the reserve price not having been met, the auction is cancelled. Thank you, ladies and gentlemen.
What will happen now?
Only three of them in it, two builders and a dark horse from London. But the house will go cheap because of its bad reputation.
Bored with the speculation, I made my excuses and headed up towards the moorlands. And that's when I first saw Ellie...

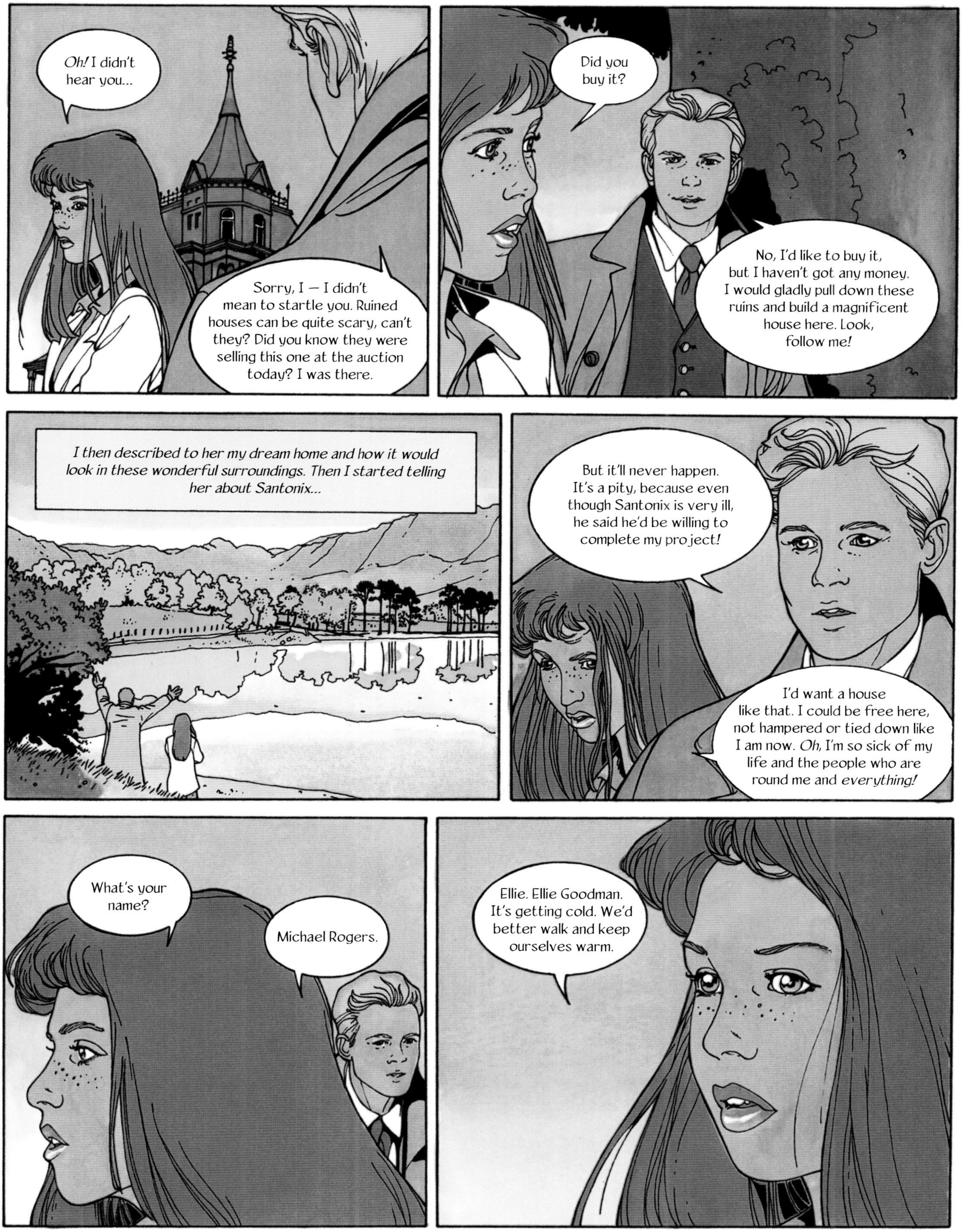
Oh! I didn't hear you...
Sorry, I — I didn't mean to startle you. Ruined houses can be quite scary, can't they? Did you know they were selling this one at the auction today? I was there.
Did you buy it?
No, I'd like to buy it, but I haven't got any money. I would gladly pull down these ruins and build a magnificent house here. Look, follow me!
I then described to her my dream home and how it would look in these wonderful surroundings. Then I started telling her about Santonix...
But it'll never happen. It's a pity, because even though Santonix is very ill, he said he'd be willing to complete my project!
I'd want a house like that. I could be free here, not hampered or tied down like I am now. *Oh*, I'm so sick of my life and the people who are round me and *everything!*
What's your name?
Michael Rogers.
Ellie. Ellie Goodman. It's getting cold. We'd better walk and keep ourselves warm.

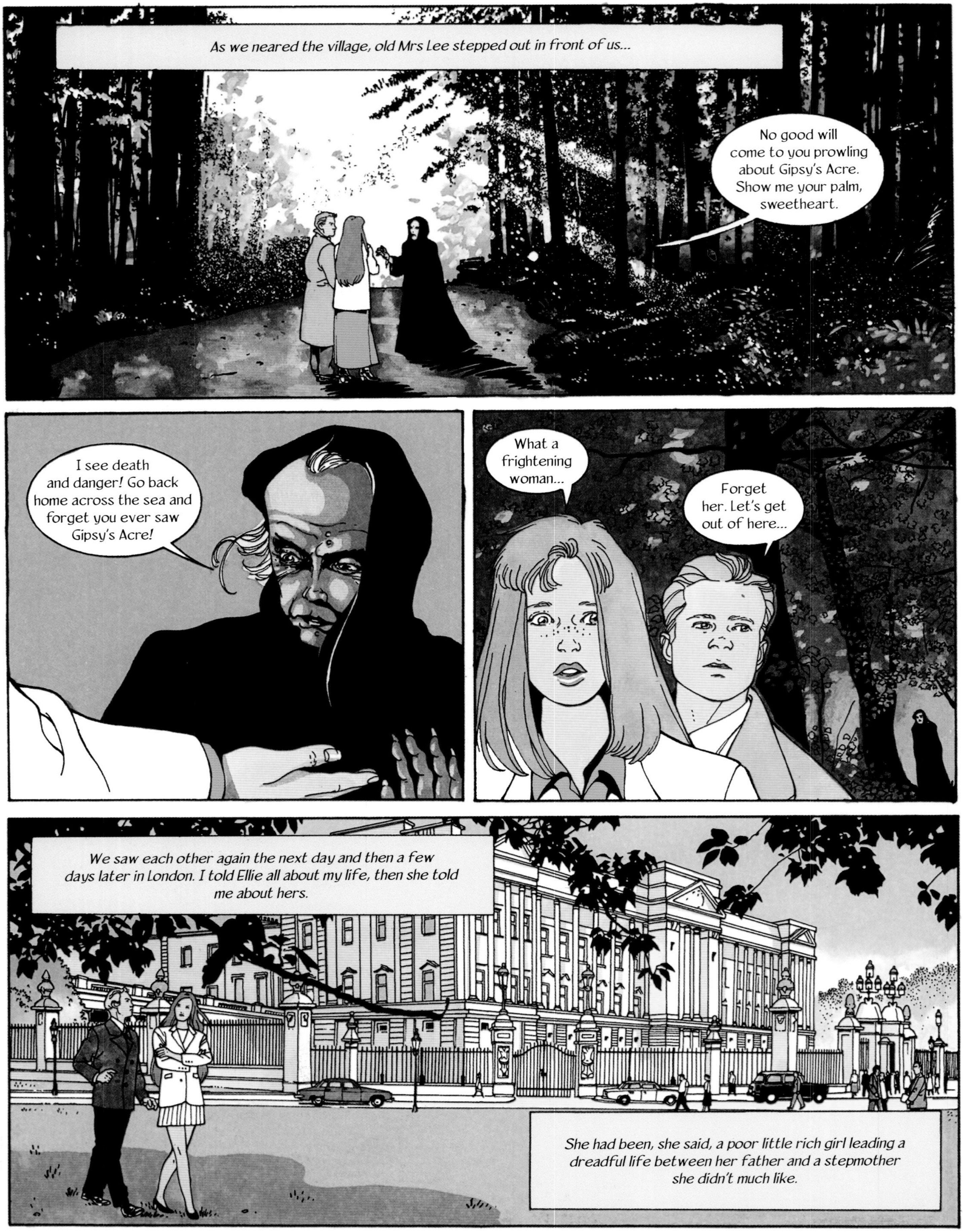
As we neared the village, old Mrs Lee stepped out in front of us...
No good will come to you prowling about Gipsy's Acre. Show me your palm, sweetheart.
I see death and danger! Go back home across the sea and forget you ever saw Gipsy's Acre!
What a frightening woman...
Forget her. Let's get out of here...
We saw each other again the next day and then a few days later in London. I told Ellie all about my life, then she told me about hers.
She had been, she said, a poor little rich girl leading a dreadful life between her father and a stepmother she didn't much like.

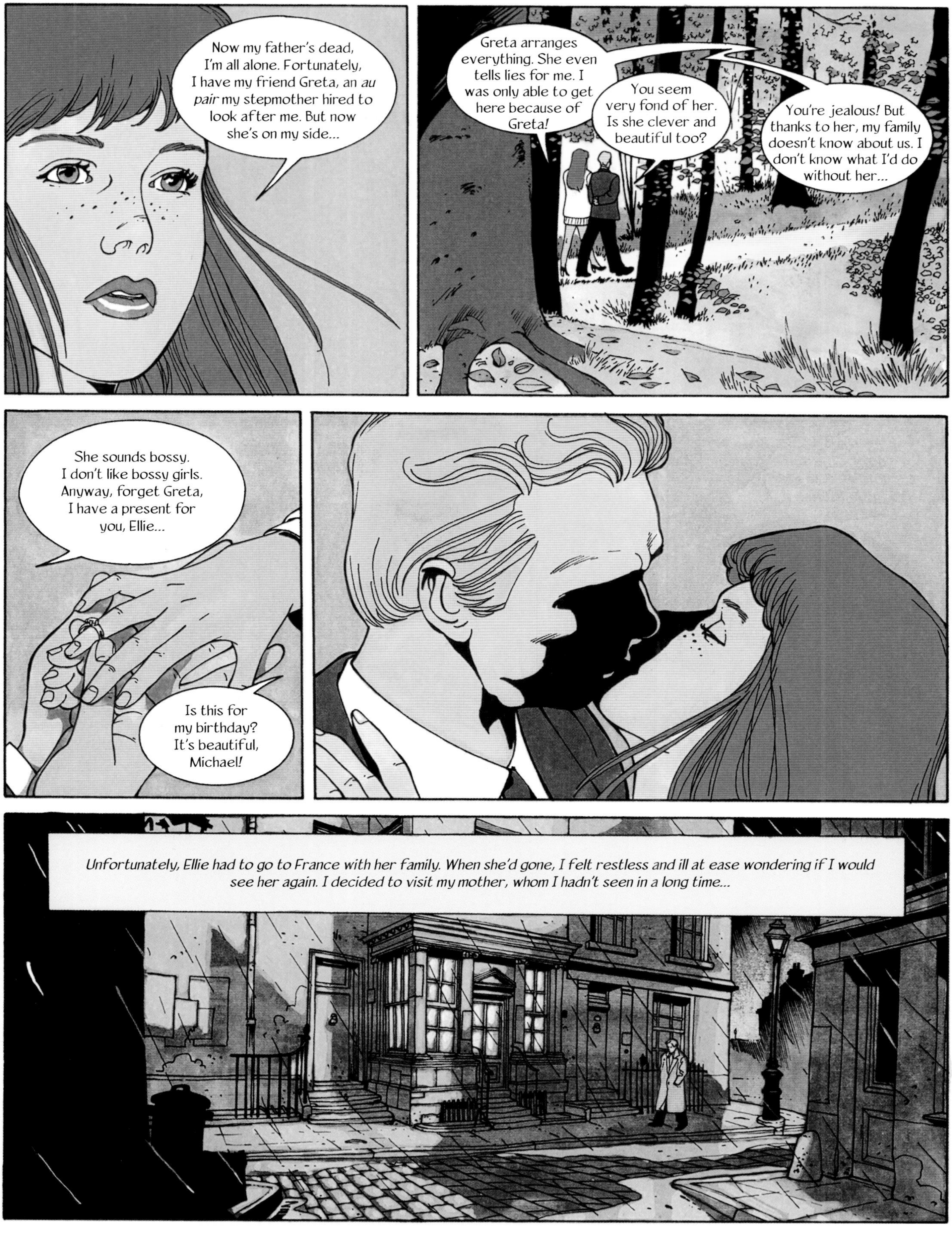
Now my father's dead, I'm all alone. Fortunately, I have my friend Greta, an *au pair* my stepmother hired to look after me. But now she's on my side...
Greta arranges everything. She even tells lies for me. I was only able to get here because of Greta!
You seem very fond of her. Is she clever and beautiful too?
You're jealous! But thanks to her, my family doesn't know about us. I don't know what I'd do without her...
She sounds bossy. I don't like bossy girls. Anyway, forget Greta, I have a present for you, Ellie...
Is this for my birthday? It's beautiful, Michael!
Unfortunately, Ellie had to go to France with her family. When she'd gone, I felt restless and ill at ease wondering if I would see her again. I decided to visit my mother, whom I hadn't seen in a long time...

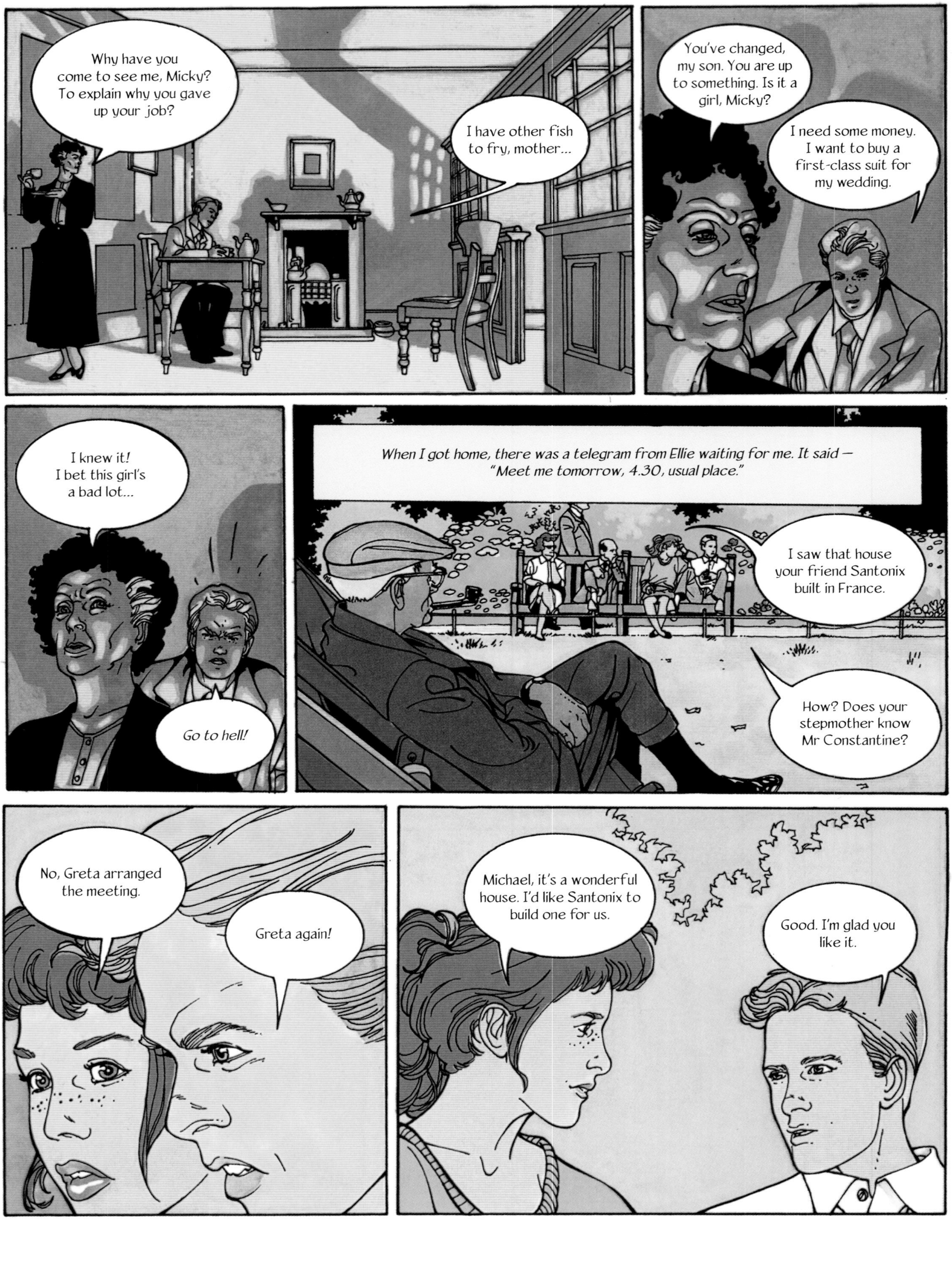
Why have you come to see me, Micky? To explain why you gave up your job?
I have other fish to fry, mother...
You've changed, my son. You are up to something. Is it a girl, Micky?
I need some money. I want to buy a first-class suit for my wedding.
I knew it! I bet this girl's a bad lot...
Go to hell!
When I got home, there was a telegram from Ellie waiting for me. It said — "Meet me tomorrow, 4.30, usual place."
I saw that house your friend Santonix built in France.
How? Does your stepmother know Mr Constantine?
No, Greta arranged the meeting.
Greta again!
Michael, it's a wonderful house. I'd like Santonix to build one for us.
Good. I'm glad you like it.

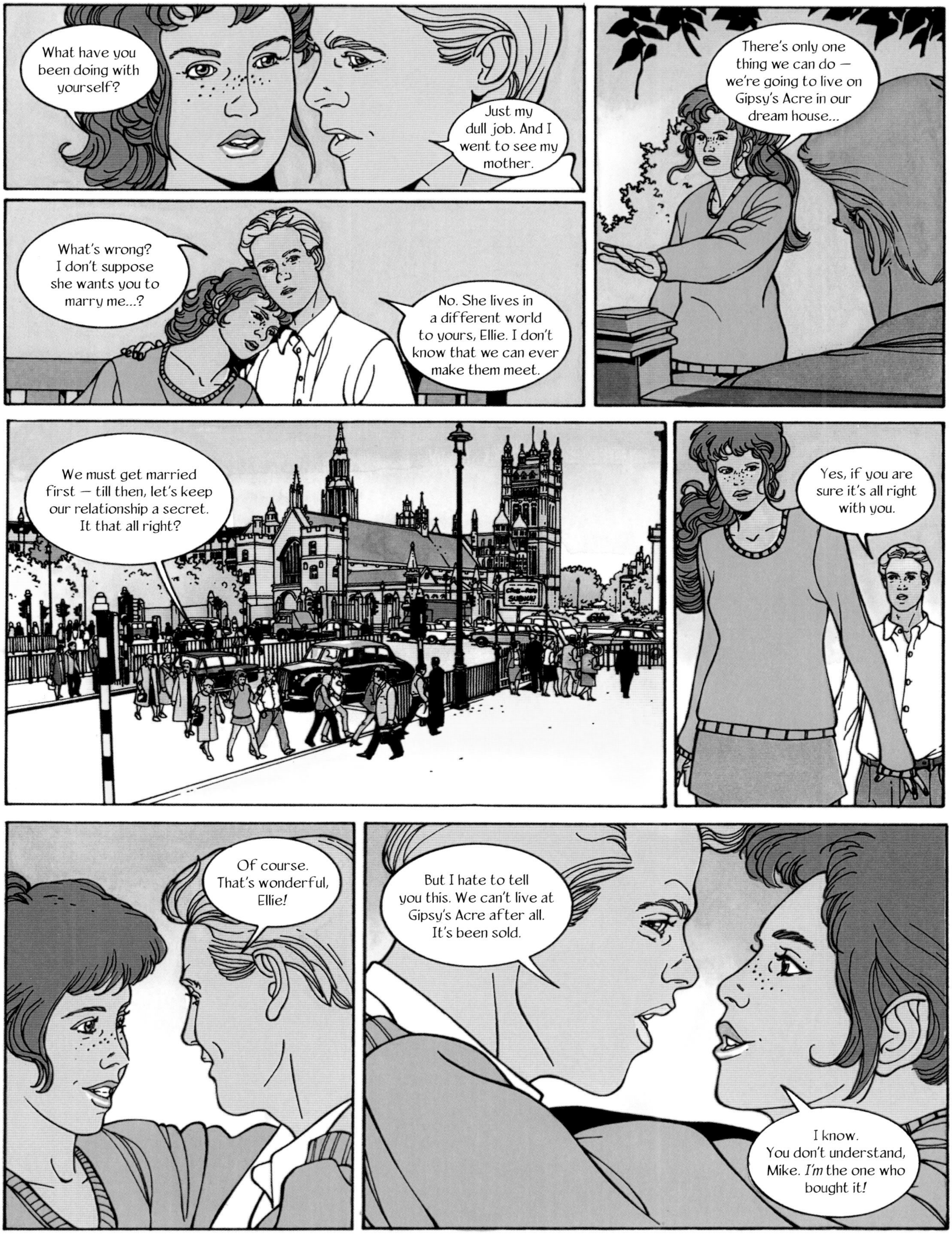
What have you been doing with yourself?
Just my dull job. And I went to see my mother.
What's wrong? I don't suppose she wants you to marry me...?
No. She lives in a different world to yours, Ellie. I don't know that we can ever make them meet.
There's only one thing we can do — we're going to live on Gipsy's Acre in our dream house...
We must get married first — till then, let's keep our relationship a secret. It that all right?
Yes, if you are sure it's all right with you.
Of course. That's wonderful, Ellie!
But I hate to tell you this. We can't live at Gipsy's Acre after all. It's been sold.
I know. You don't understand, Mike. *I'm* the one who bought it!

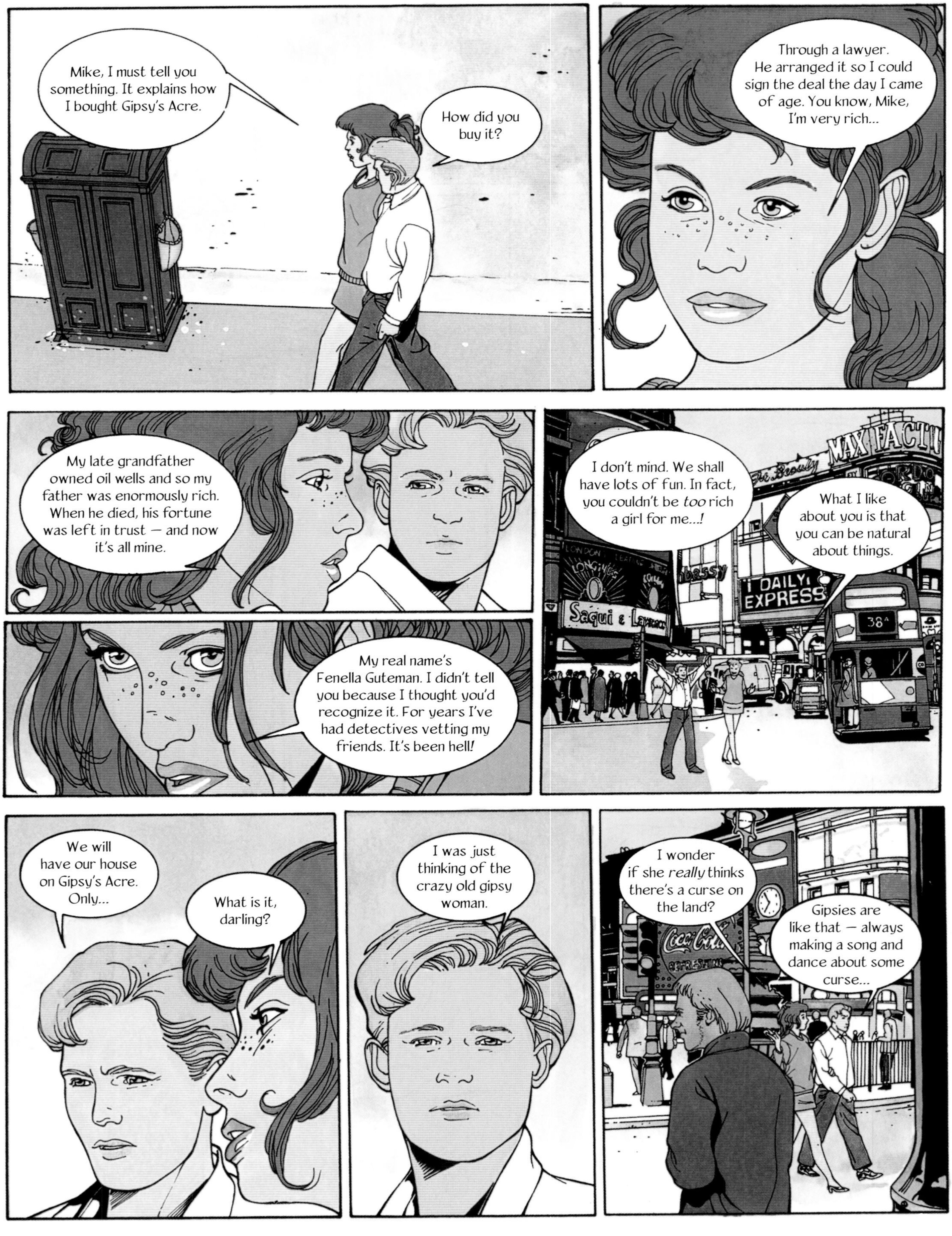
Mike, I must tell you something. It explains how I bought Gipsy's Acre.
How did you buy it?
Through a lawyer. He arranged it so I could sign the deal the day I came of age. You know, Mike, I'm very rich...
My late grandfather owned oil wells and so my father was enormously rich. When he died, his fortune was left in trust — and now it's all mine.
My real name's Fenella Guteman. I didn't tell you because I thought you'd recognize it. For years I've had detectives vetting my friends. It's been hell!
MAX FACTO
DAILY EXPRESS
Saqui & Lawrence
38A
I don't mind. We shall have lots of fun. In fact, you couldn't be *too* rich a girl for me...!
What I like about you is that you can be natural about things.
We will have our house on Gipsy's Acre. Only...
What is it, darling?
I was just thinking of the crazy old gipsy woman.
I wonder if she *really* thinks there's a curse on the land?
Gipsies are like that — always making a song and dance about some curse...

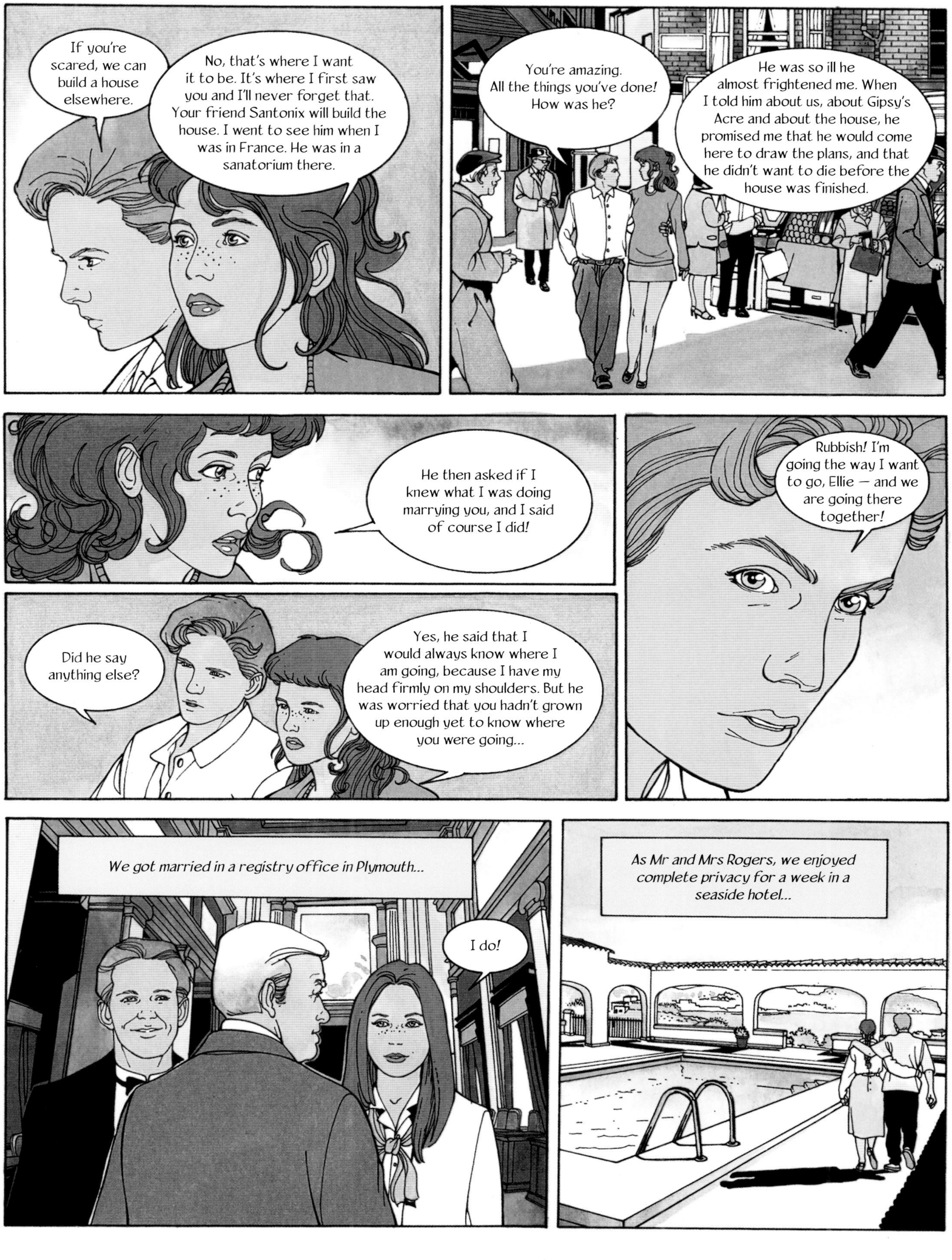

If you're scared, we can build a house elsewhere.
No, that's where I want it to be. It's where I first saw you and I'll never forget that. Your friend Santonix will build the house. I went to see him when I was in France. He was in a sanatorium there.
You're amazing. All the things you've done! How was he?
He was so ill he almost frightened me. When I told him about us, about Gipsy's Acre and about the house, he promised me that he would come here to draw the plans, and that he didn't want to die before the house was finished.
He then asked if I knew what I was doing marrying you, and I said of course I did!
Rubbish! I'm going the way I want to go, Ellie — and we are going there together!
Did he say anything else?
Yes, he said that I would always know where I am going, because I have my head firmly on my shoulders. But he was worried that you hadn't grown up enough yet to know where you were going...
We got married in a registry office in Plymouth...
I do!
As Mr and Mrs Rogers, we enjoyed complete privacy for a week in a seaside hotel...

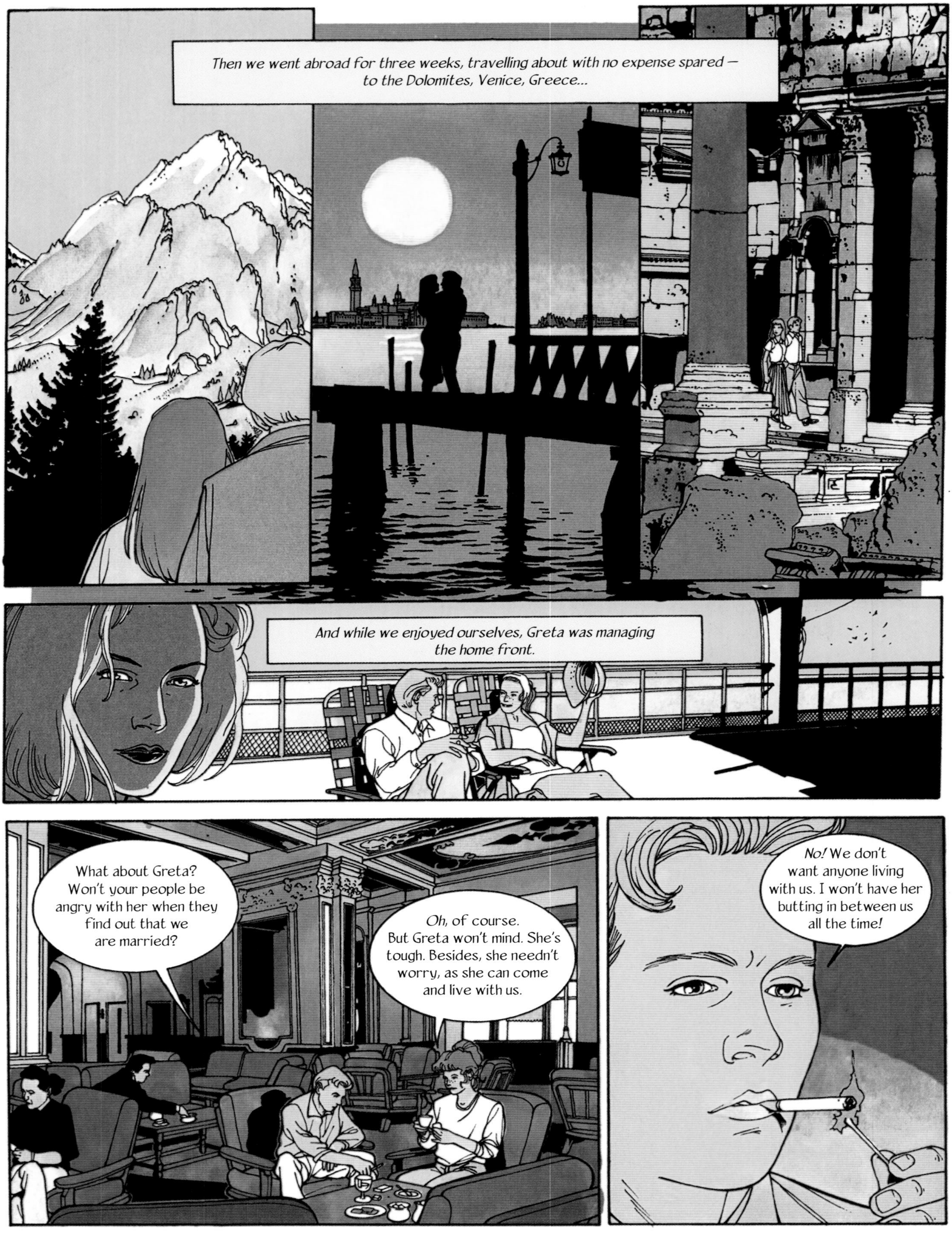
Then we went abroad for three weeks, travelling about with no expense spared — to the Dolomites, Venice, Greece...
And while we enjoyed ourselves, Greta was managing the home front.
What about Greta? Won't your people be angry with her when they find out that we are married?
Oh, of course. But Greta won't mind. She's tough. Besides, she needn't worry, as she can come and live with us.
No! We don't want anyone living with us. I won't have her butting in between us all the time!

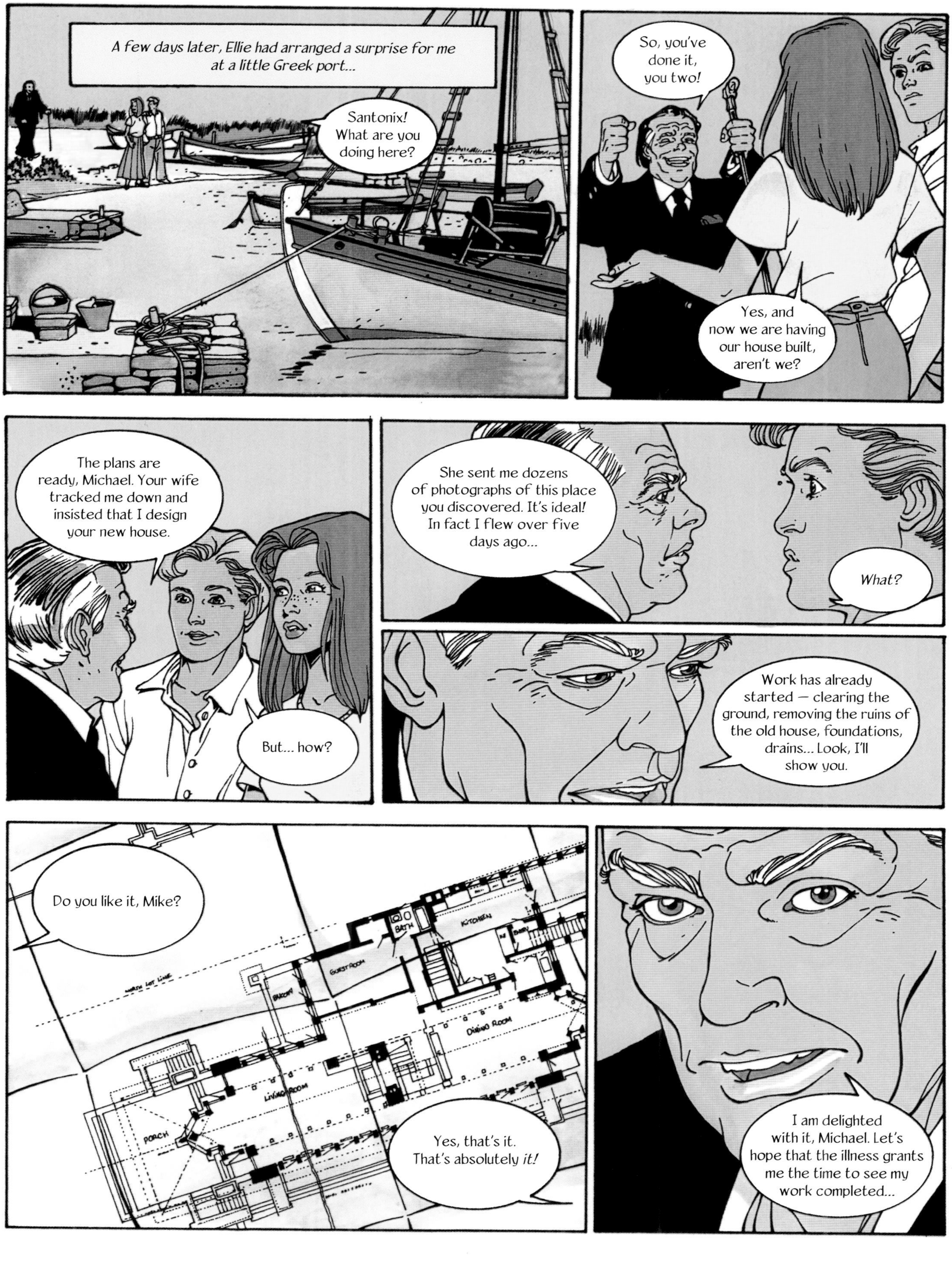
A few days later, Ellie had arranged a surprise for me at a little Greek port...
Santonix! What are you doing here?
So, you've done it, you two!
Yes, and now we are having our house built, aren't we?
The plans are ready, Michael. Your wife tracked me down and insisted that I design your new house.
But... how?
She sent me dozens of photographs of this place you discovered. It's ideal! In fact I flew over five days ago...
What?
Work has already started — clearing the ground, removing the ruins of the old house, foundations, drains... Look, I'll show you.
Do you like it, Mike?
KITCHEN
BATH
GUEST ROOM
DINING ROOM
LIVING ROOM
PORCH
Yes, that's it. That's absolutely *it!*
I am delighted with it, Michael. Let's hope that the illness grants me the time to see my work completed...

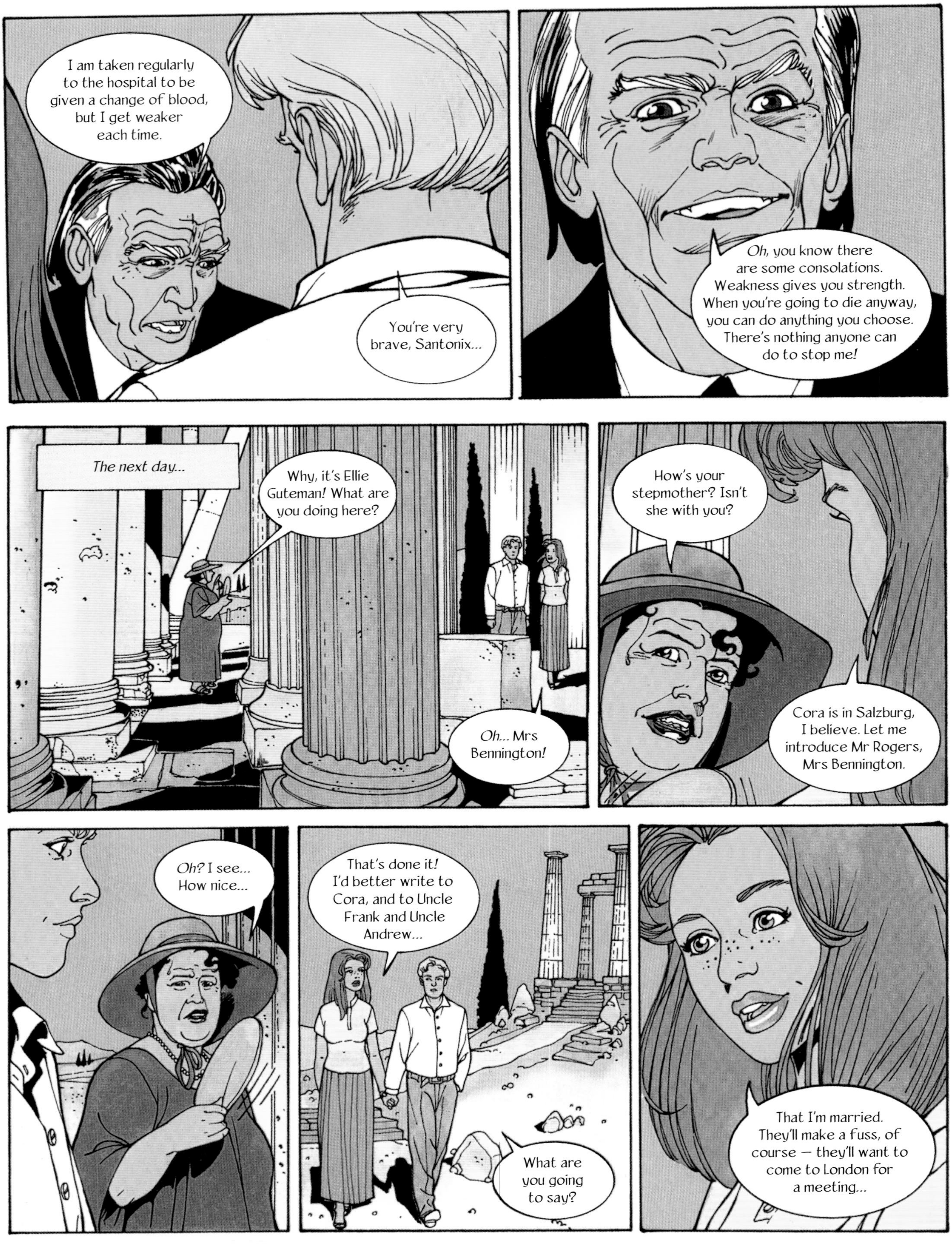
I am taken regularly to the hospital to be given a change of blood, but I get weaker each time.
You're very brave, Santonix...
Oh, you know there are some consolations. Weakness gives you strength. When you're going to die anyway, you can do anything you choose. There's nothing anyone can do to stop me*!*
The next day...
Why, it's Ellie Guteman*!* What are you doing here?
Oh... Mrs Bennington*!*
How's your stepmother? Isn't she with you?
Cora is in Salzburg, I believe. Let me introduce Mr Rogers, Mrs Bennington.
Oh? I see... How nice...
That's done it*!* I'd better write to Cora, and to Uncle Frank and Uncle Andrew...
What are you going to say?
That I'm married. They'll make a fuss, of course — they'll want to come to London for a meeting...

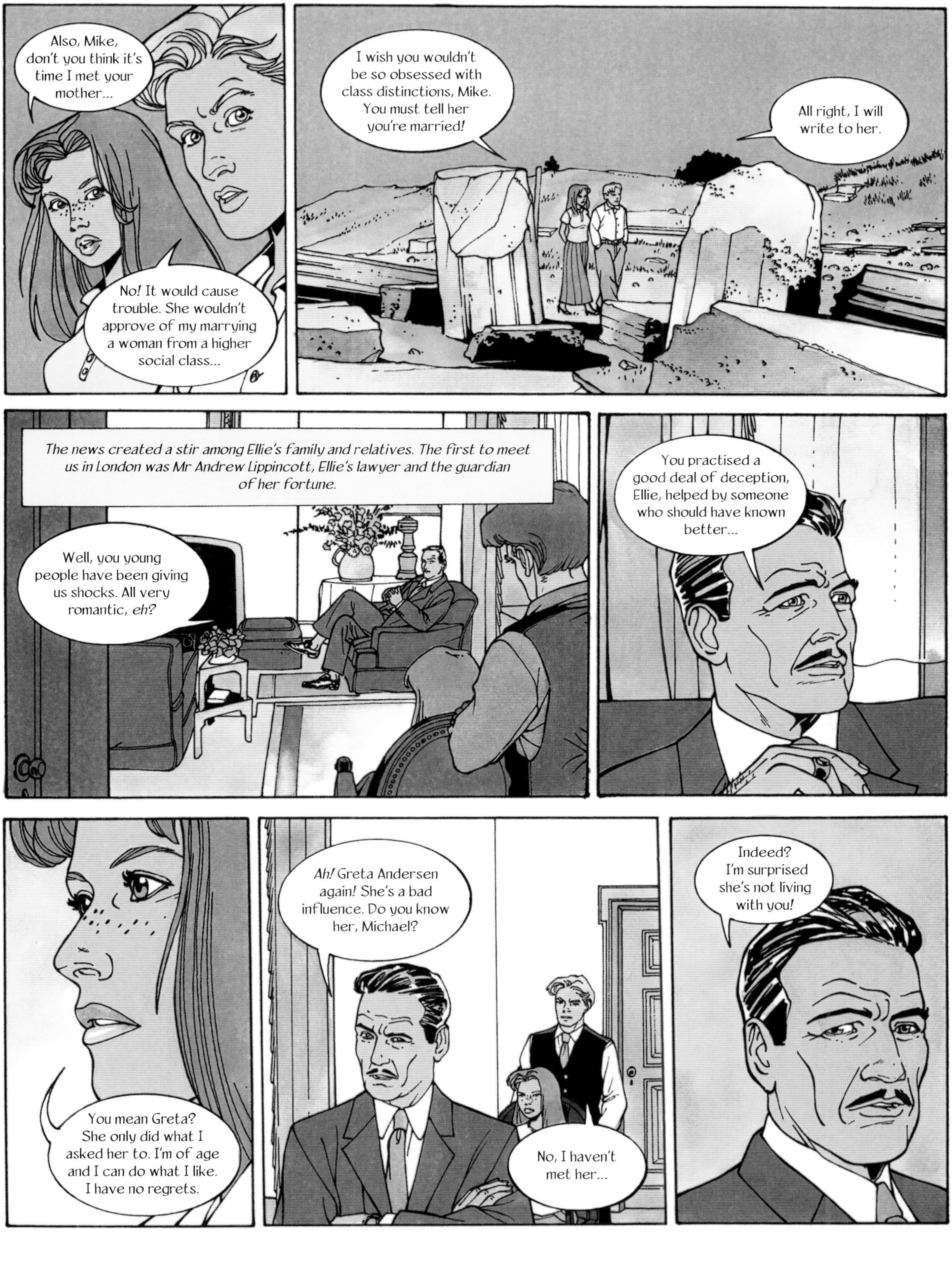
Also, Mike, don't you think it's time I met your mother...
No! It would cause trouble. She wouldn't approve of my marrying a woman from a higher social class...
I wish you wouldn't be so obsessed with class distinctions, Mike. You must tell her you're married!
All right, I will write to her.
The news created a stir among Ellie's family and relatives. The first to meet us in London was Mr Andrew Lippincott, Ellie's lawyer and the guardian of her fortune.
Well, you young people have been giving us shocks. All very romantic, *eh?*
You practised a good deal of deception, Ellie, helped by someone who should have known better...
You mean Greta? She only did what I asked her to. I'm of age and I can do what I like. I have no regrets.
Ah! Greta Andersen again! She's a bad influence. Do you know her, Michael?
No, I haven't met her...
Indeed? I'm surprised she's not living with you*!*

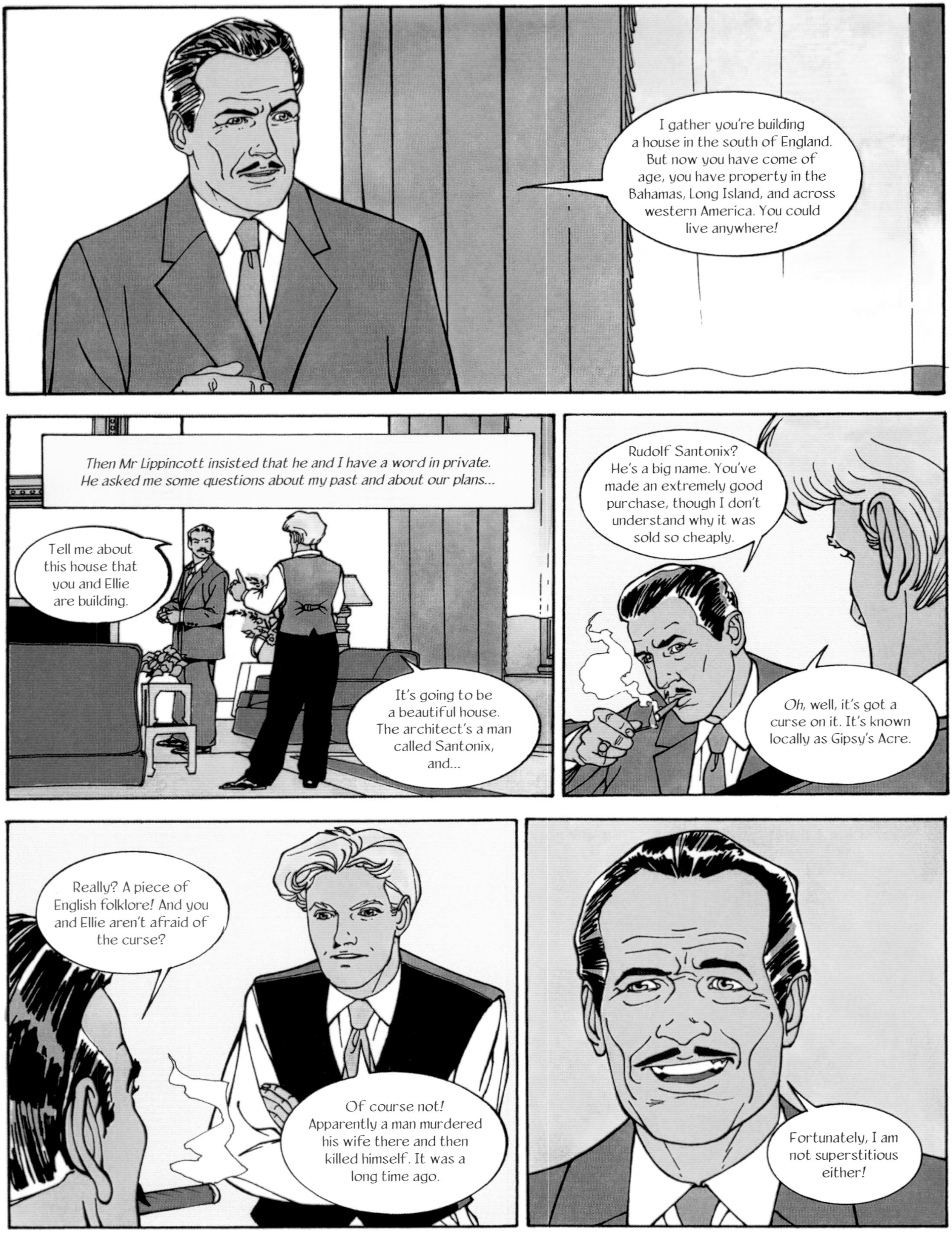

I gather you're building a house in the south of England. But now you have come of age, you have property in the Bahamas, Long Island, and across western America. You could live anywhere!
Then Mr Lippincott insisted that he and I have a word in private. He asked me some questions about my past and about our plans...
Tell me about this house that you and Ellie are building.
It's going to be a beautiful house. The architect's a man called Santonix, and...
Rudolf Santonix? He's a big name. You've made an extremely good purchase, though I don't understand why it was sold so cheaply.
Oh, well, it's got a curse on it. It's known locally as Gipsy's Acre.
Really? A piece of English folklore! And you and Ellie aren't afraid of the curse?
Of course not! Apparently a man murdered his wife there and then killed himself. It was a long time ago.
Fortunately, I am not superstitious either!

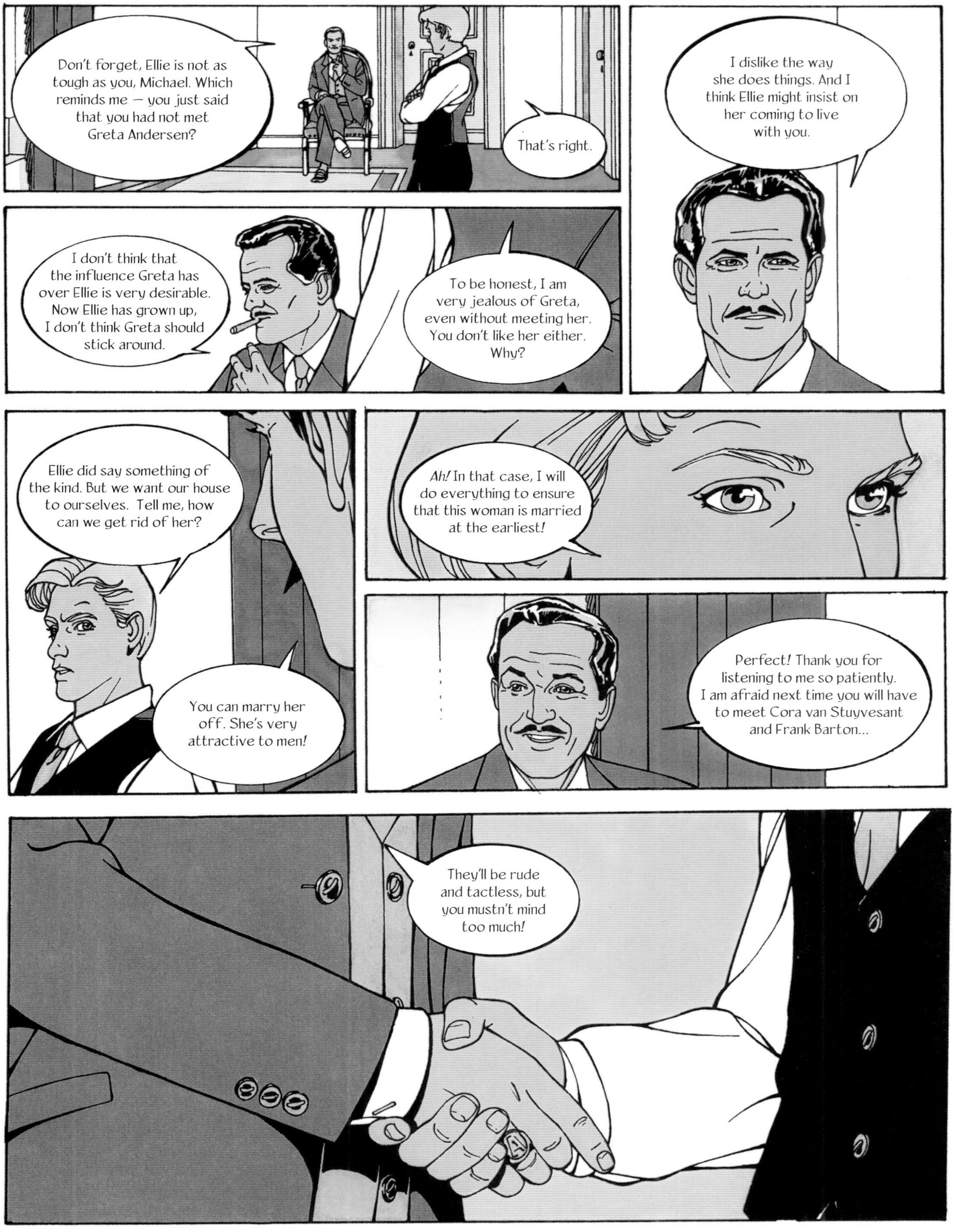
Don't forget, Ellie is not as tough as you, Michael. Which reminds me — you just said that you had not met Greta Andersen?
That's right.
I dislike the way she does things. And I think Ellie might insist on her coming to live with you.
I don't think that the influence Greta has over Ellie is very desirable. Now Ellie has grown up, I don't think Greta should stick around.
To be honest, I am very jealous of Greta, even without meeting her. You don't like her either. Why?
Ellie did say something of the kind. But we want our house to ourselves. Tell me, how can we get rid of her?
You can marry her off. She's very attractive to men!
Ah! In that case, I will do everything to ensure that this woman is married at the earliest!
Perfect! Thank you for listening to me so patiently. I am afraid next time you will have to meet Cora van Stuyvesant and Frank Barton...
They'll be rude and tactless, but you mustn't mind too much!

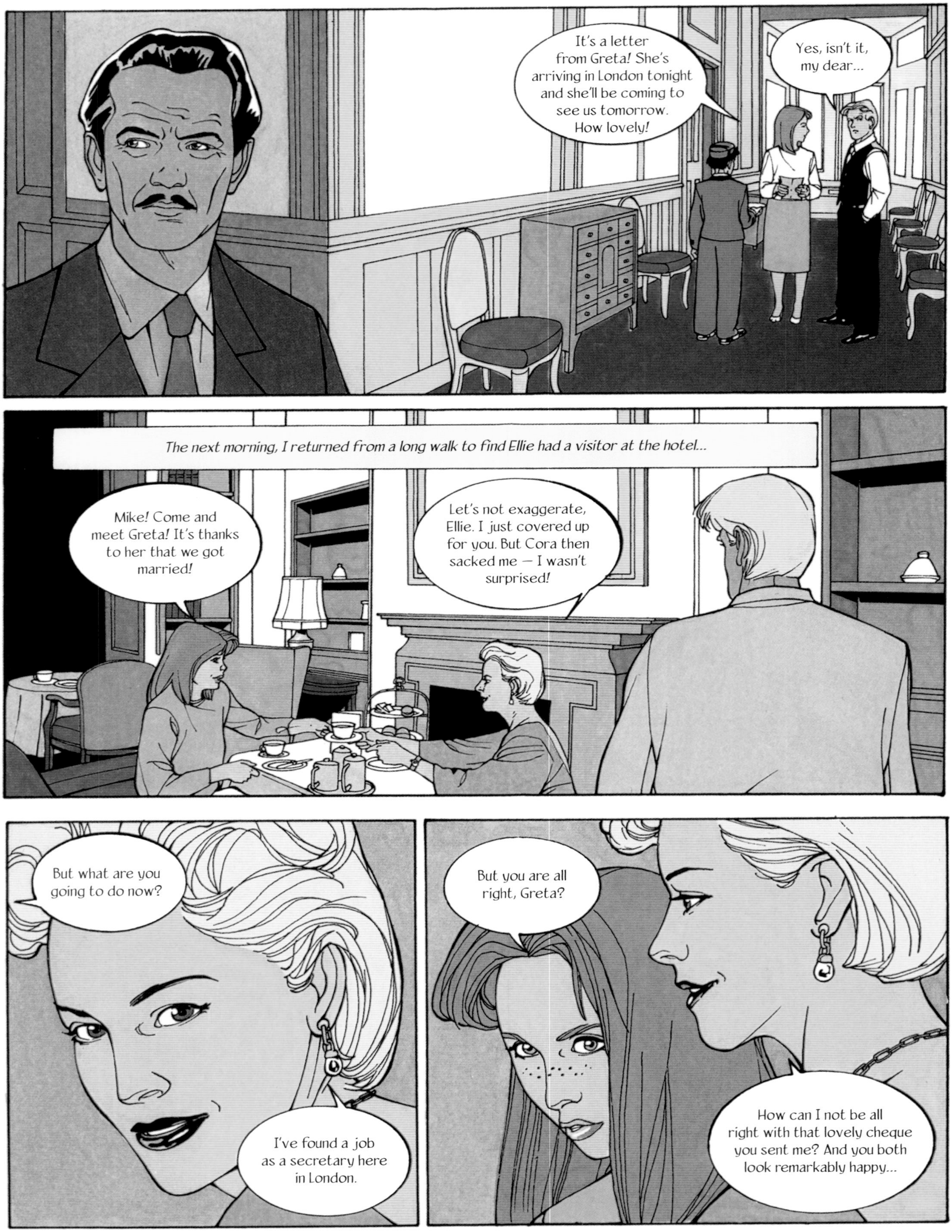
It's a letter from Greta! She's arriving in London tonight and she'll be coming to see us tomorrow. How lovely!
Yes, isn't it, my dear...
The next morning, I returned from a long walk to find Ellie had a visitor at the hotel...
Mike! Come and meet Greta! It's thanks to her that we got married!
Let's not exaggerate, Ellie. I just covered up for you. But Cora then sacked me — I wasn't surprised!
But what are you going to do now?
I've found a job as a secretary here in London.
But you are all right, Greta?
How can I not be all right with that lovely cheque you sent me? And you both look remarkably happy...

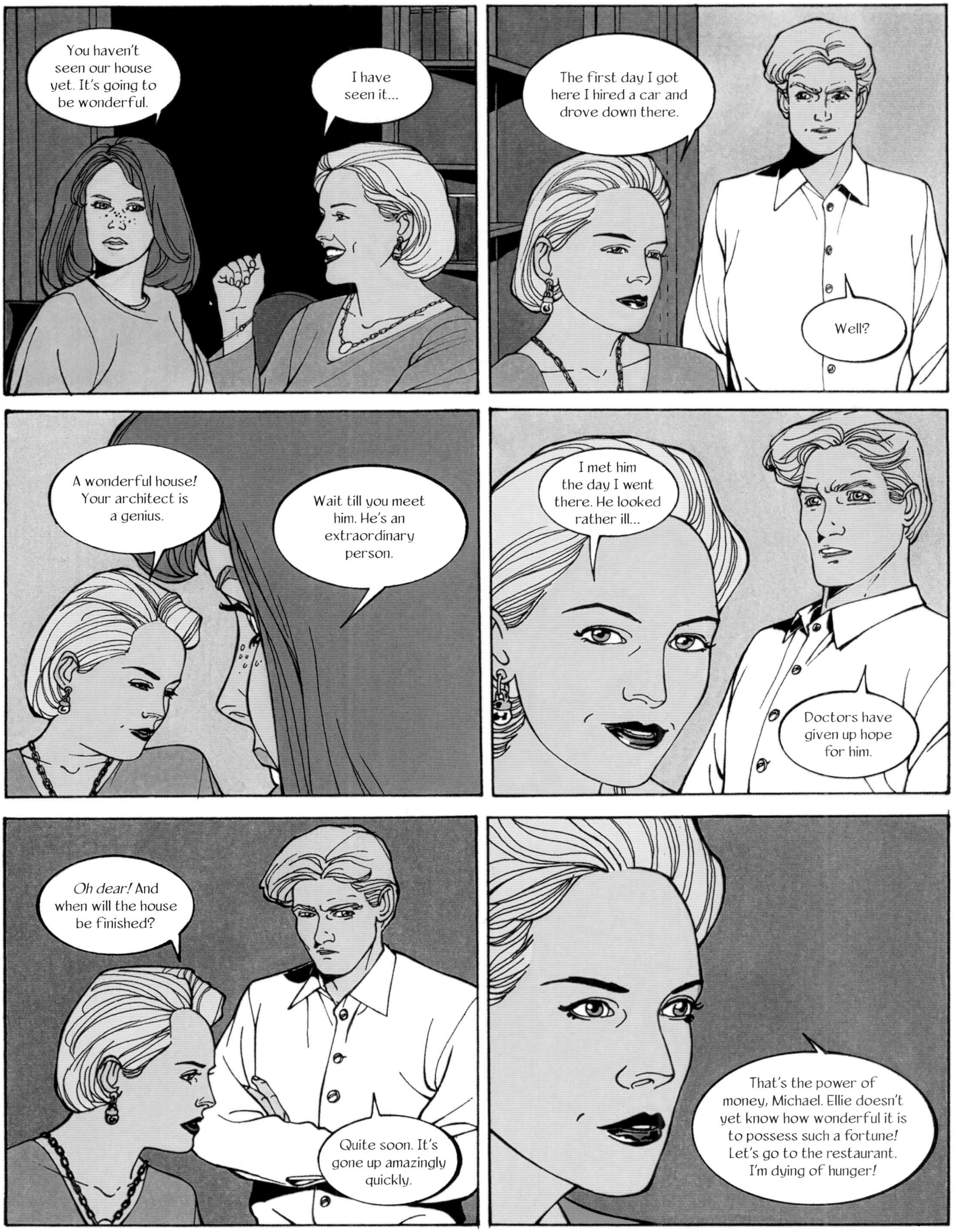
You haven't seen our house yet. It's going to be wonderful.
I have seen it...
The first day I got here I hired a car and drove down there.
Well?
A wonderful house! Your architect is a genius.
Wait till you meet him. He's an extraordinary person.
I met him the day I went there. He looked rather ill...
Doctors have given up hope for him.
Oh dear! And when will the house be finished?
Quite soon. It's gone up amazingly quickly.
That's the power of money, Michael. Ellie doesn't yet know how wonderful it is to possess such a fortune! Let's go to the restaurant. I'm dying of hunger!

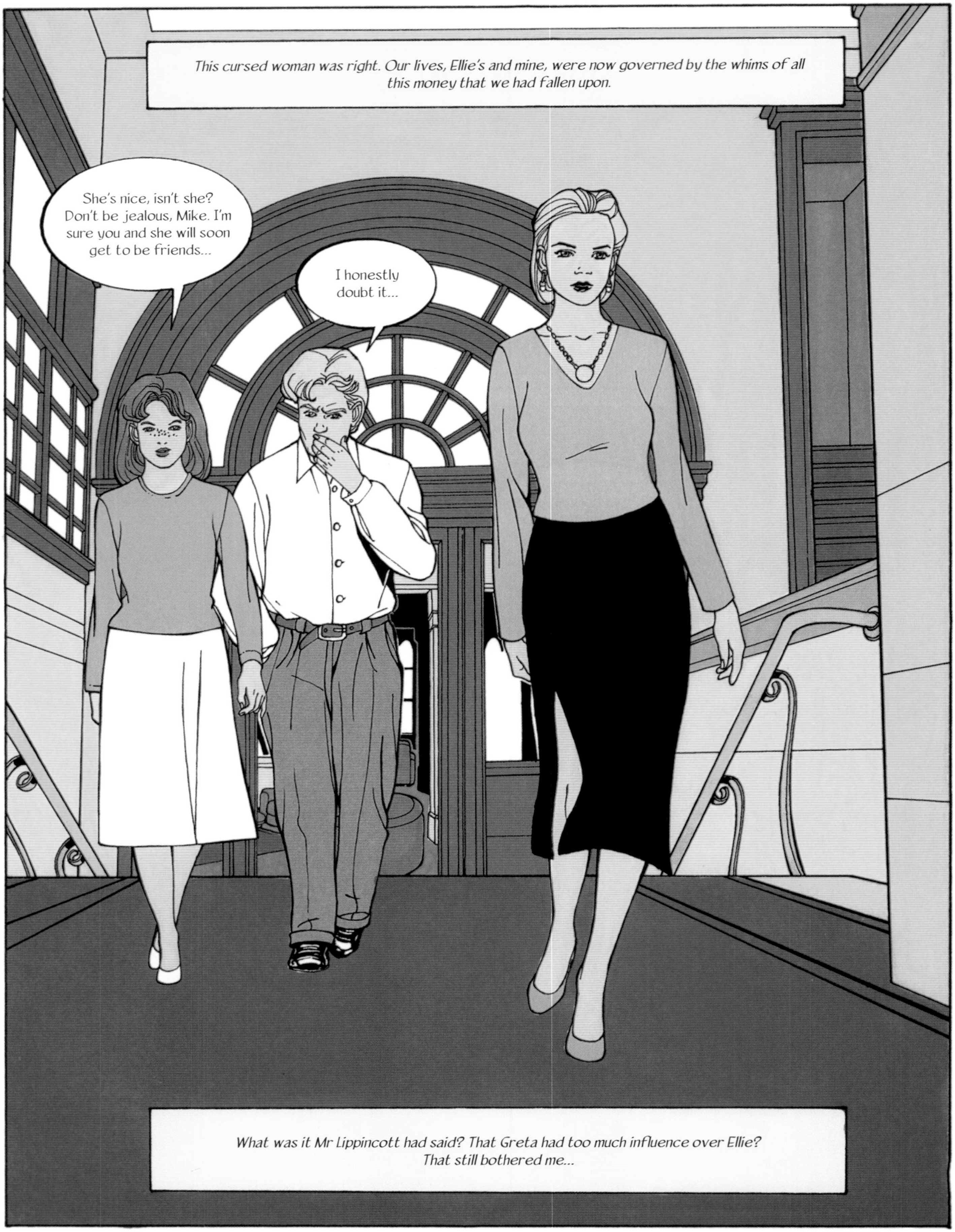
This cursed woman was right. Our lives, Ellie's and mine, were now governed by the whims of all this money that we had fallen upon.
She's nice, isn't she? Don't be jealous, Mike. I'm sure you and she will soon get to be friends...
I honestly doubt it...
What was it Mr Lippincott had said? That Greta had too much influence over Ellie? That still bothered me...

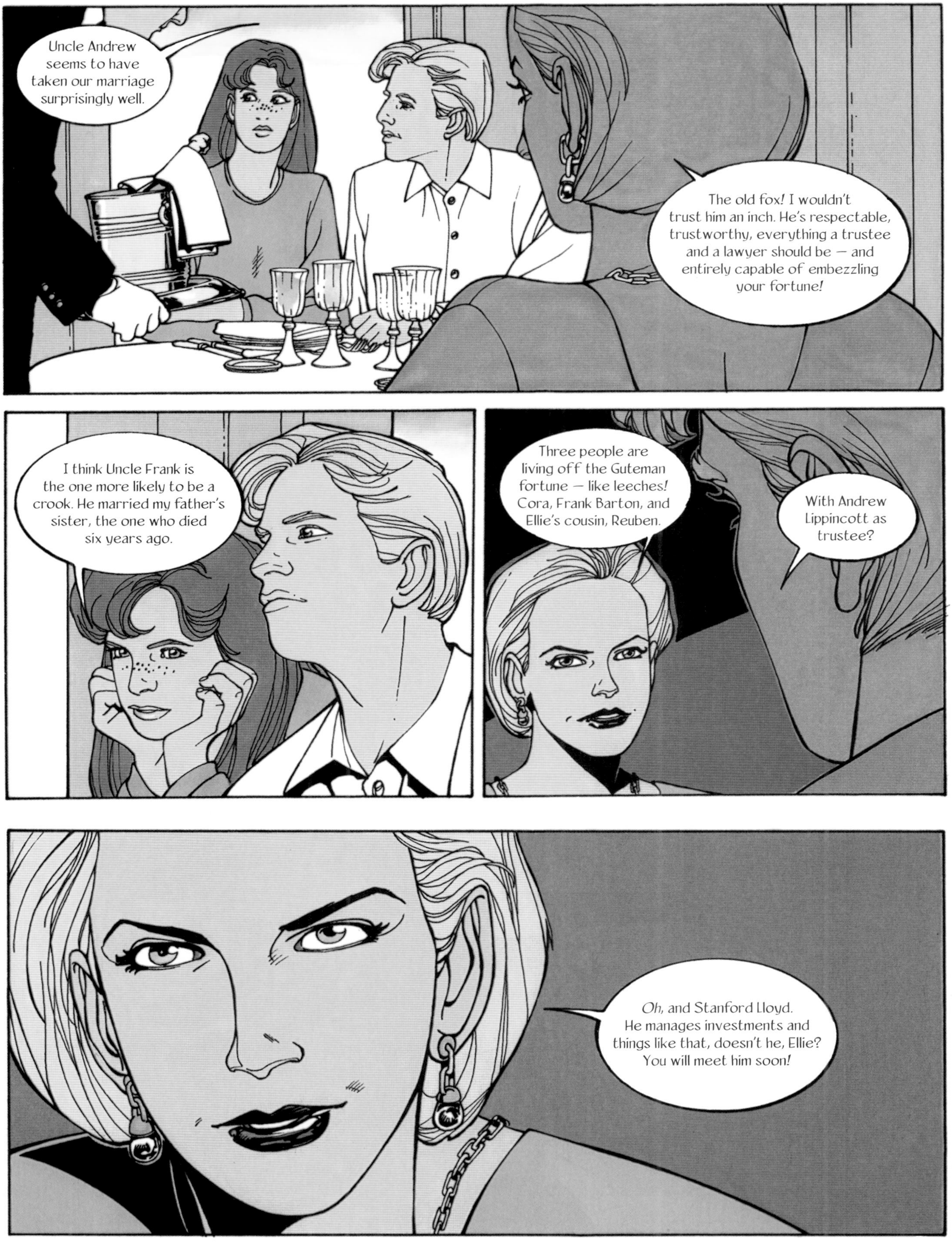
Uncle Andrew seems to have taken our marriage surprisingly well.
The old fox! I wouldn't trust him an inch. He's respectable, trustworthy, everything a trustee and a lawyer should be — and entirely capable of embezzling your fortune!
I think Uncle Frank is the one more likely to be a crook. He married my father's sister, the one who died six years ago.
Three people are living off the Guteman fortune — like leeches! Cora, Frank Barton, and Ellie's cousin, Reuben.
With Andrew Lippincott as trustee?
Oh, and Stanford Lloyd. He manages investments and things like that, doesn't he, Ellie? You will meet him soon!

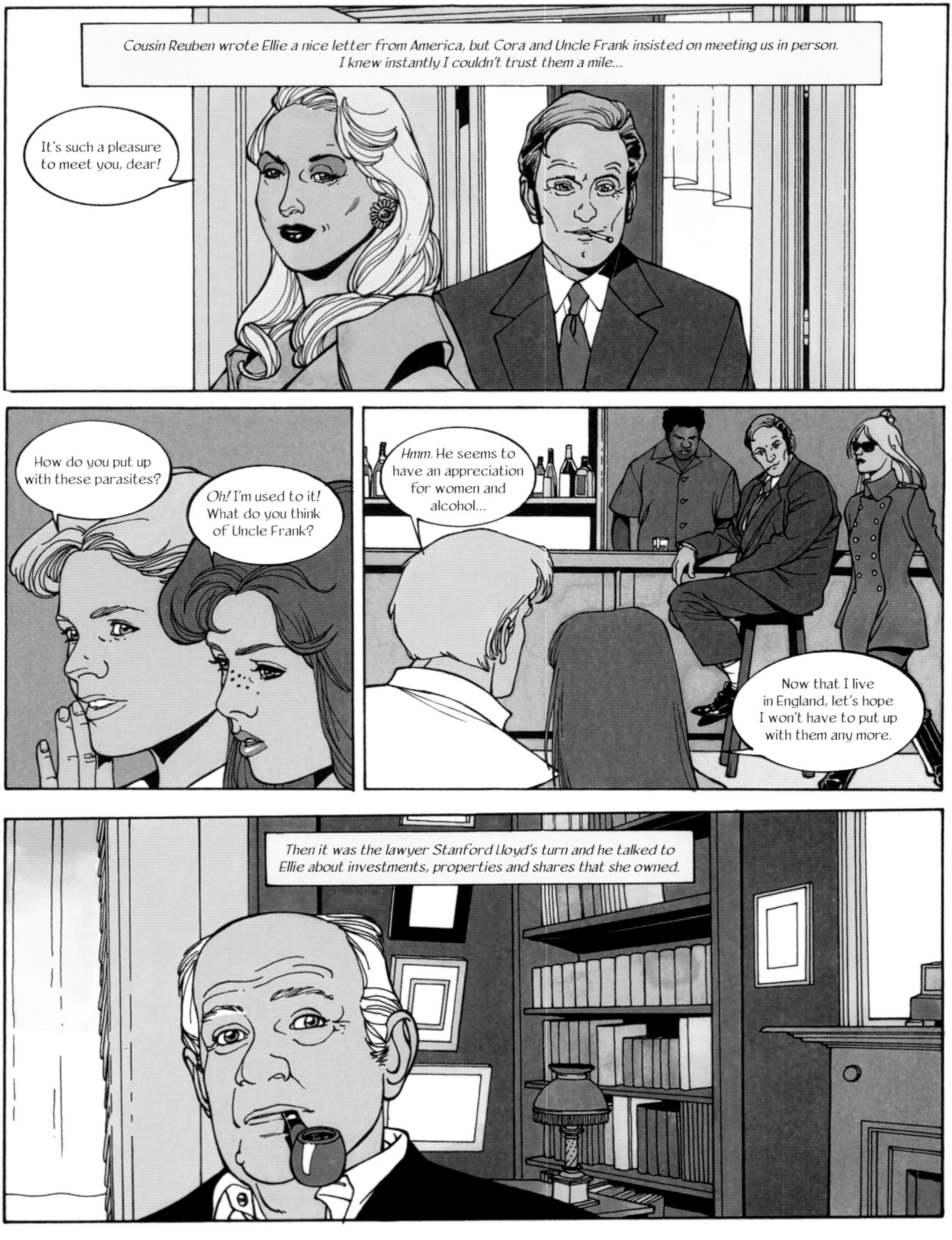

Cousin Reuben wrote Ellie a nice letter from America, but Cora and Uncle Frank insisted on meeting us in person. I knew instantly I couldn't trust them a mile...
It's such a pleasure to meet you, dear!
How do you put up with these parasites?
Oh! I'm used to it! What do you think of Uncle Frank?
Hmm. He seems to have an appreciation for women and alcohol...
Now that I live in England, let's hope I won't have to put up with them any more.
Then it was the lawyer Stanford Lloyd's turn and he talked to Ellie about investments, properties and shares that she owned.

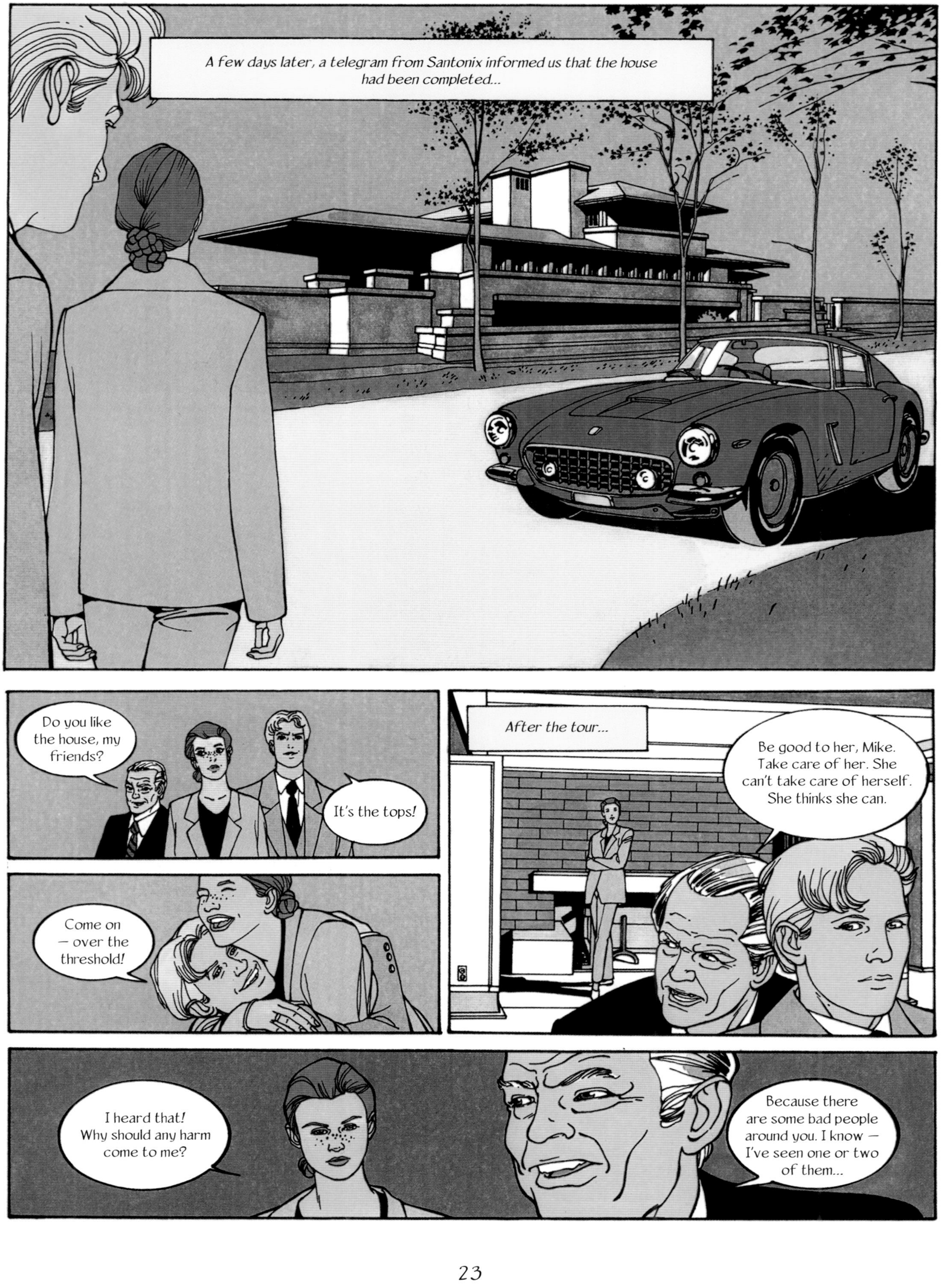
A few days later, a telegram from Santonix informed us that the house had been completed...
Do you like the house, my friends?
It's the tops!
Come on — over the threshold!
After the tour...
Be good to her, Mike. Take care of her. She can't take care of herself. She thinks she can.
I heard that! Why should any harm come to me?
Because there are some bad people around you. I know — I've seen one or two of them...

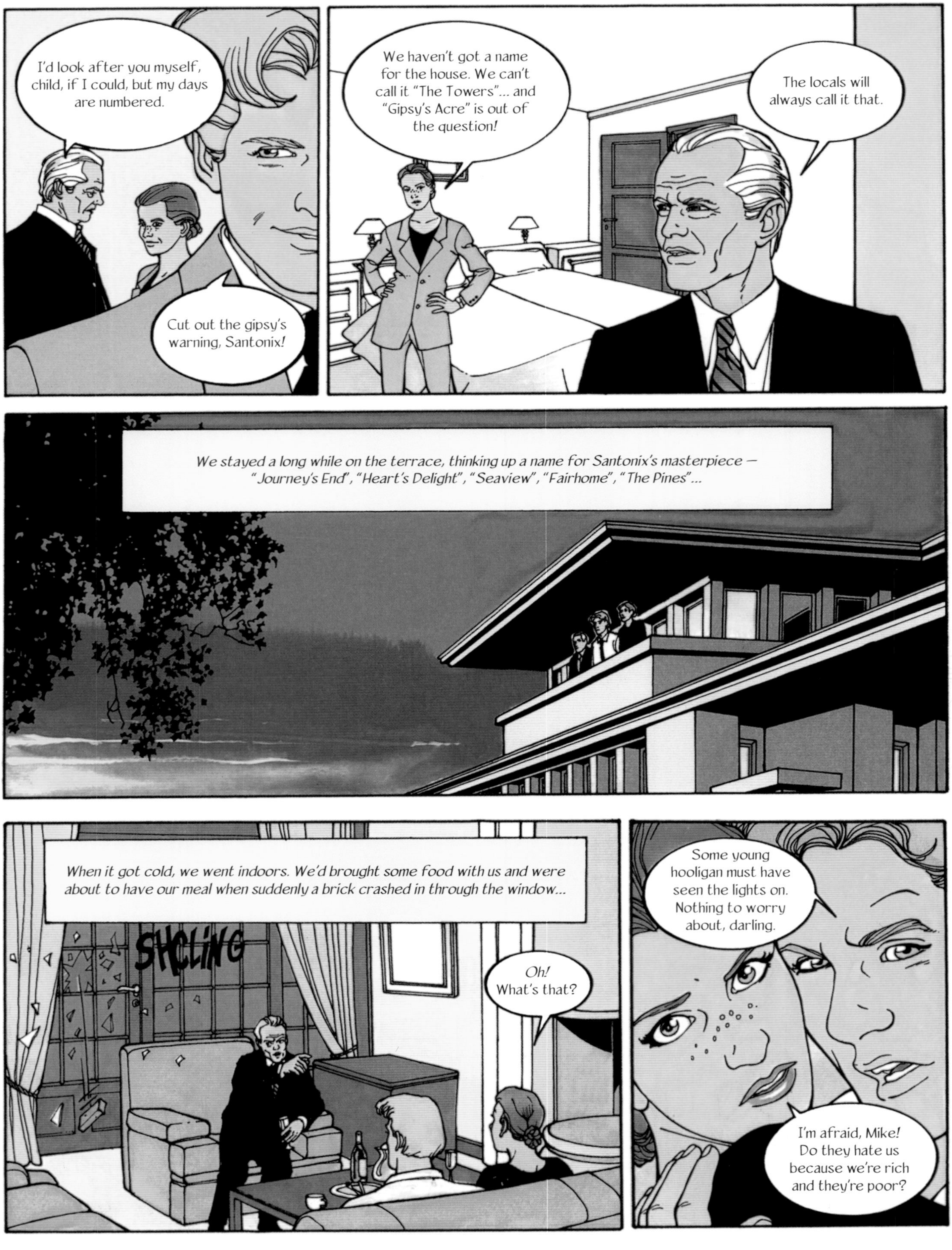
I'd look after you myself, child, if I could, but my days are numbered.
Cut out the gipsy's warning, Santonix!
We haven't got a name for the house. We can't call it "The Towers"... and "Gipsy's Acre" is out of the question!
The locals will always call it that.
We stayed a long while on the terrace, thinking up a name for Santonix's masterpiece — "Journey's End", "Heart's Delight", "Seaview", "Fairhome", "The Pines"...
When it got cold, we went indoors. We'd brought some food with us and were about to have our meal when suddenly a brick crashed in through the window...
SHCLING
Oh! What's that?
Some young hooligan must have seen the lights on. Nothing to worry about, darling.
I'm afraid, Mike! Do they hate us because we're rich and they're poor?

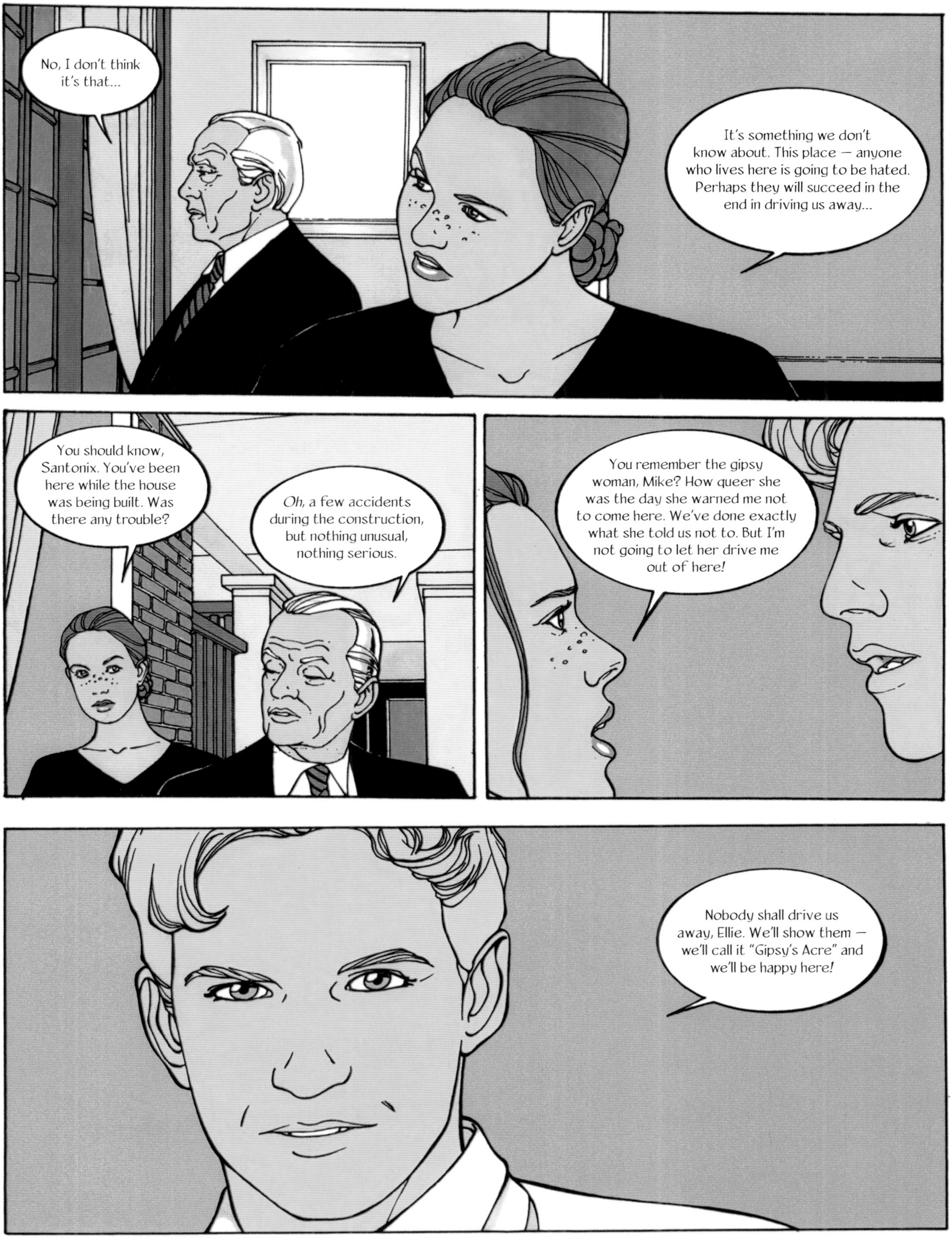
No, I don't think it's that...
It's something we don't know about. This place — anyone who lives here is going to be hated. Perhaps they will succeed in the end in driving us away...
You should know, Santonix. You've been here while the house was being built. Was there any trouble?
Oh, a few accidents during the construction, but nothing unusual, nothing serious.
You remember the gipsy woman, Mike? How queer she was the day she warned me not to come here. We've done exactly what she told us not to. But I'm not going to let her drive me out of here!
Nobody shall drive us away, Ellie. We'll show them — we'll call it "Gipsy's Acre" and we'll be happy here!

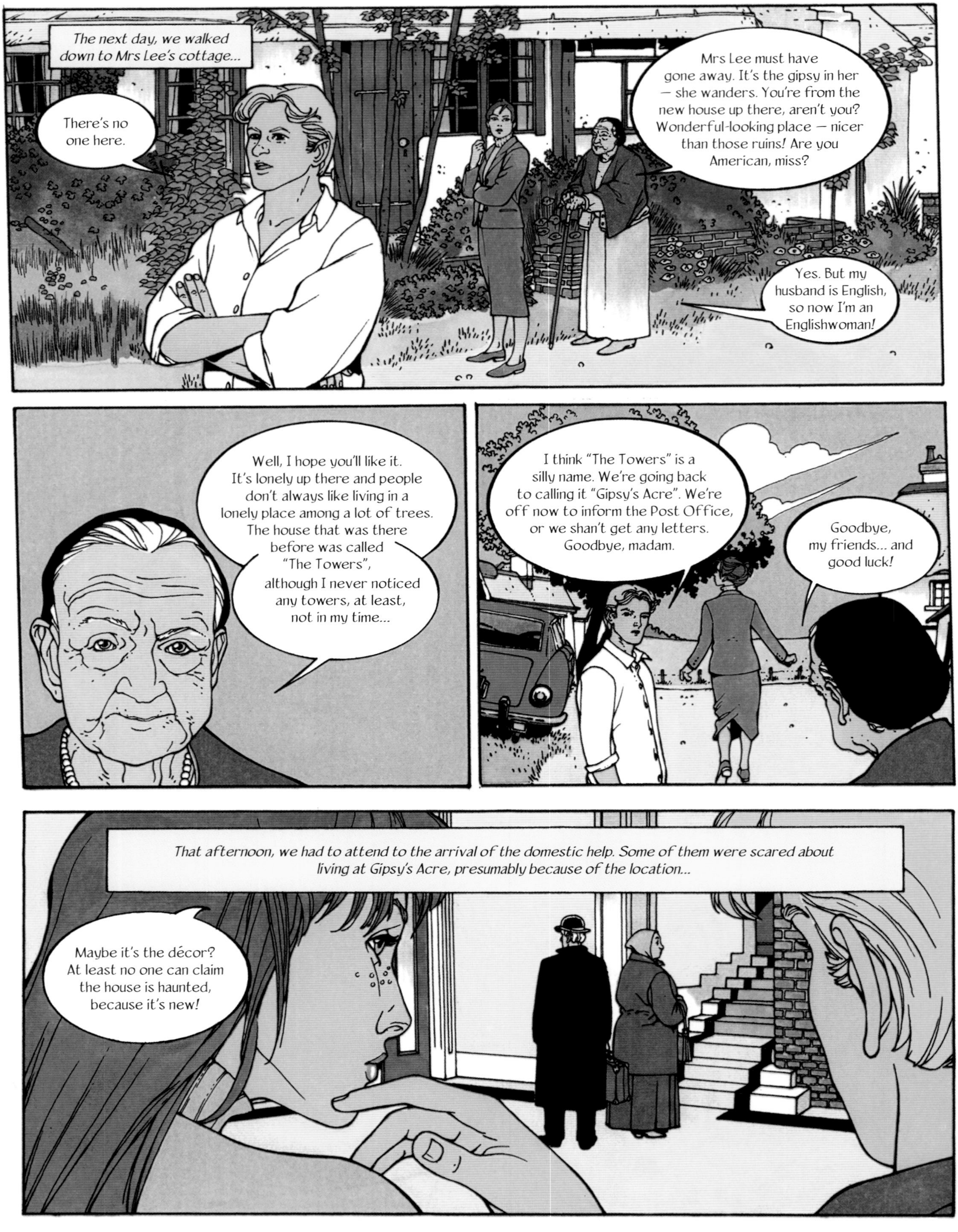
The next day, we walked down to Mrs Lee's cottage...
There's no one here.
Mrs Lee must have gone away. It's the gipsy in her — she wanders. You're from the new house up there, aren't you? Wonderful-looking place — nicer than those ruins! Are you American, miss?
Yes. But my husband is English, so now I'm an Englishwoman!
Well, I hope you'll like it. It's lonely up there and people don't always like living in a lonely place among a lot of trees. The house that was there before was called "The Towers", although I never noticed any towers, at least, not in my time...
I think "The Towers" is a silly name. We're going back to calling it "Gipsy's Acre". We're off now to inform the Post Office, or we shan't get any letters. Goodbye, madam.
Goodbye, my friends... and good luck!
That afternoon, we had to attend to the arrival of the domestic help. Some of them were scared about living at Gipsy's Acre, presumably because of the location...
Maybe it's the décor? At least no one can claim the house is haunted, because it's new!

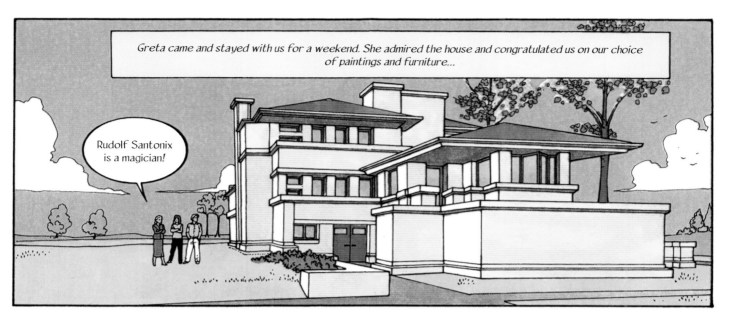

Greta came and stayed with us for a weekend. She admired the house and congratulated us on our choice of paintings and furniture...

Rudolf Santonix is a magician!

One afternoon, an important figure in Kingston Bishop, Major Phillpot, visited us...

My wife sent me. She's disabled. She asked me to advise you on which plants grow best around here!

I suppose you know the tales surrounding this area, my friends...?

Yes, thanks to old Mrs Lee.

Poor old Esther! She isn't as crazy as she makes out. She's been a nuisance, has she?

She only warned us against coming here!

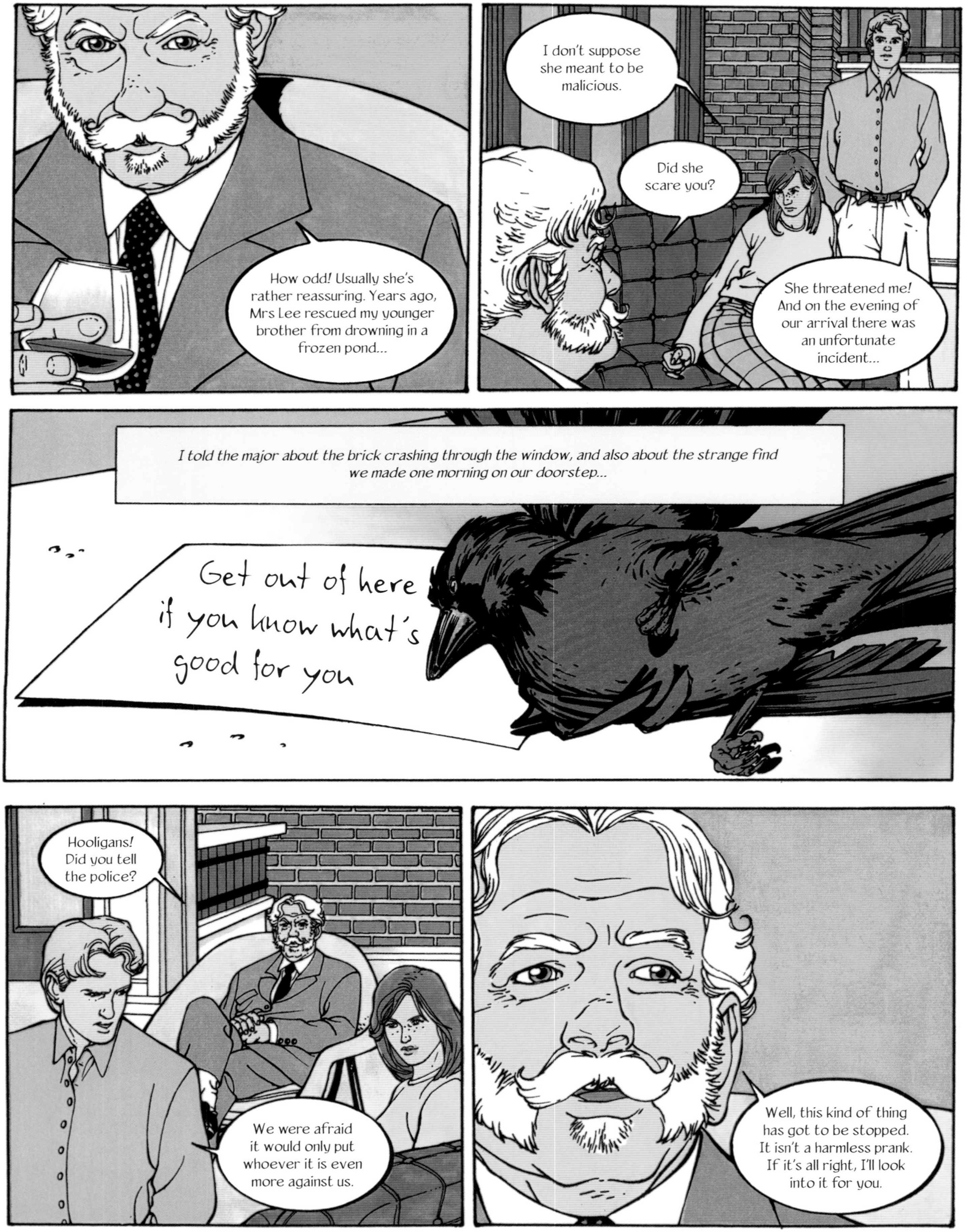
How odd! Usually she's rather reassuring. Years ago, Mrs Lee rescued my younger brother from drowning in a frozen pond...
I don't suppose she meant to be malicious.
Did she scare you?
She threatened me! And on the evening of our arrival there was an unfortunate incident...
I told the major about the brick crashing through the window, and also about the strange find we made one morning on our doorstep...
Get out of here if you know what's good for you
Hooligans! Did you tell the police?
We were afraid it would only put whoever it is even more against us.
Well, this kind of thing has got to be stopped. It isn't a harmless prank. If it's all right, I'll look into it for you.

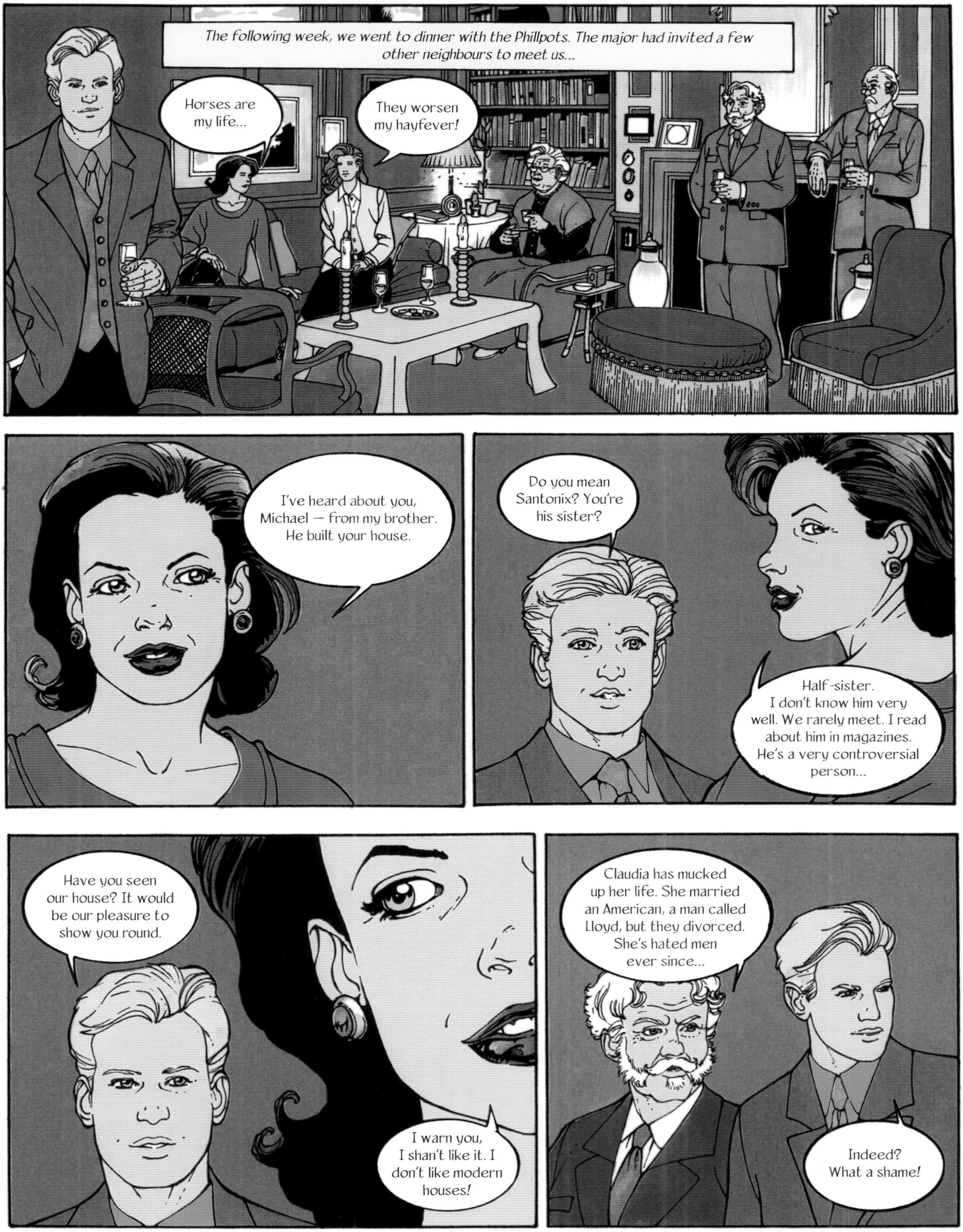
The following week, we went to dinner with the Phillpots. The major had invited a few other neighbours to meet us...
Horses are my life...
They worsen my hayfever!
I've heard about you, Michael — from my brother. He built your house.
Do you mean Santonix? You're his sister?
Half-sister. I don't know him very well. We rarely meet. I read about him in magazines. He's a very controversial person...
Have you seen our house? It would be our pleasure to show you round.
I warn you, I shan't like it. I don't like modern houses!
Claudia has mucked up her life. She married an American, a man called Lloyd, but they divorced. She's hated men ever since...
Indeed? What a shame!

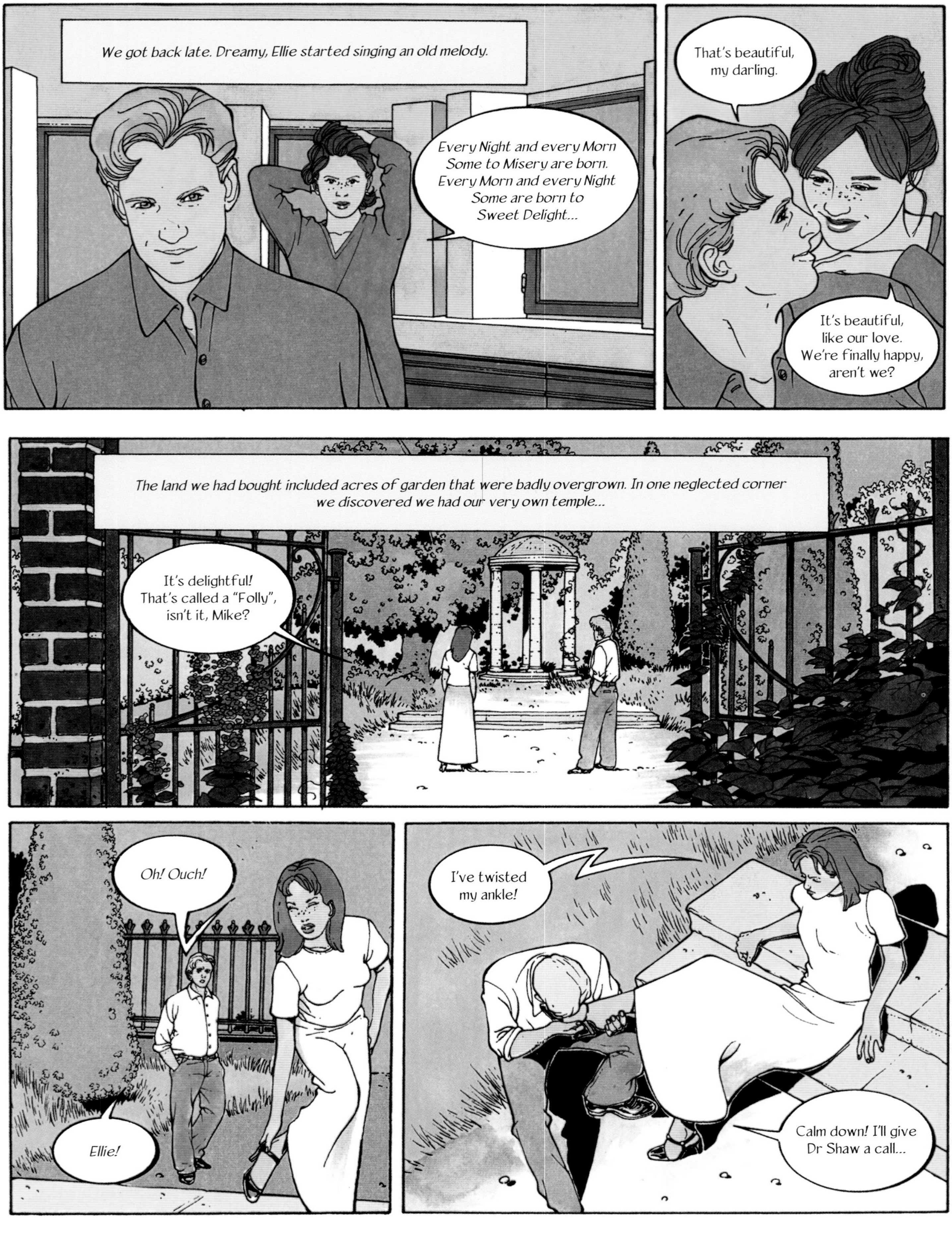
We got back late. Dreamy, Ellie started singing an old melody.
Every Night and every Morn Some to Misery are born. Every Morn and every Night Some are born to Sweet Delight...
That's beautiful, my darling.
It's beautiful, like our love. We're finally happy, aren't we?
The land we had bought included acres of garden that were badly overgrown. In one neglected corner we discovered we had our very own temple...
It's delightful! That's called a "Folly", isn't it, Mike?
Oh! Ouch!
Ellie!
I've twisted my ankle!
Calm down! I'll give Dr Shaw a call...

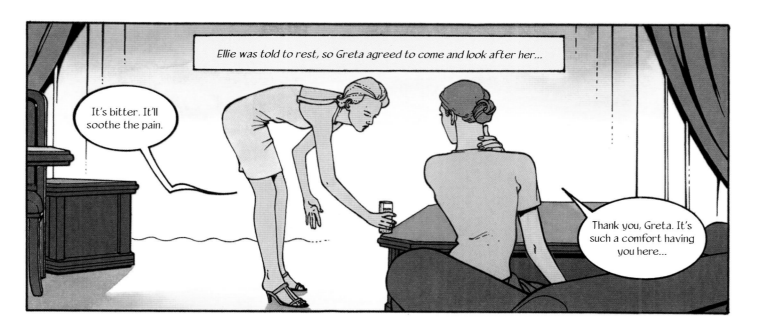

Ellie was told to rest, so Greta agreed to come and look after her...

It's bitter. It'll soothe the pain.

Thank you, Greta. It's such a comfort having you here...

But I didn't like the way this intruder started to take control of Ellie. One day, I couldn't hold back any more and I told her she was bossy and interfering...

I didn't realize that you hated her so much!

I'm sorry, I lost my temper. But it's true!

Fortunately, Ellie was making friends with the neighbours, and once her ankle had healed, she would go horse riding with Claudia Hardcastle. Then, one afternoon, I found Greta was upset...

A terrible-looking old gipsy woman planted herself in the middle of the road — made me stop the car...

She threatened me! She claimed said this is gipsy land and that our lives are in danger if we don't leave.

Damn' cheek!

I think Greta was exaggerating a bit, Ellie.

Do you think so? I saw the gipsy too when I was riding. She predicted the ruin of our home — and my death!

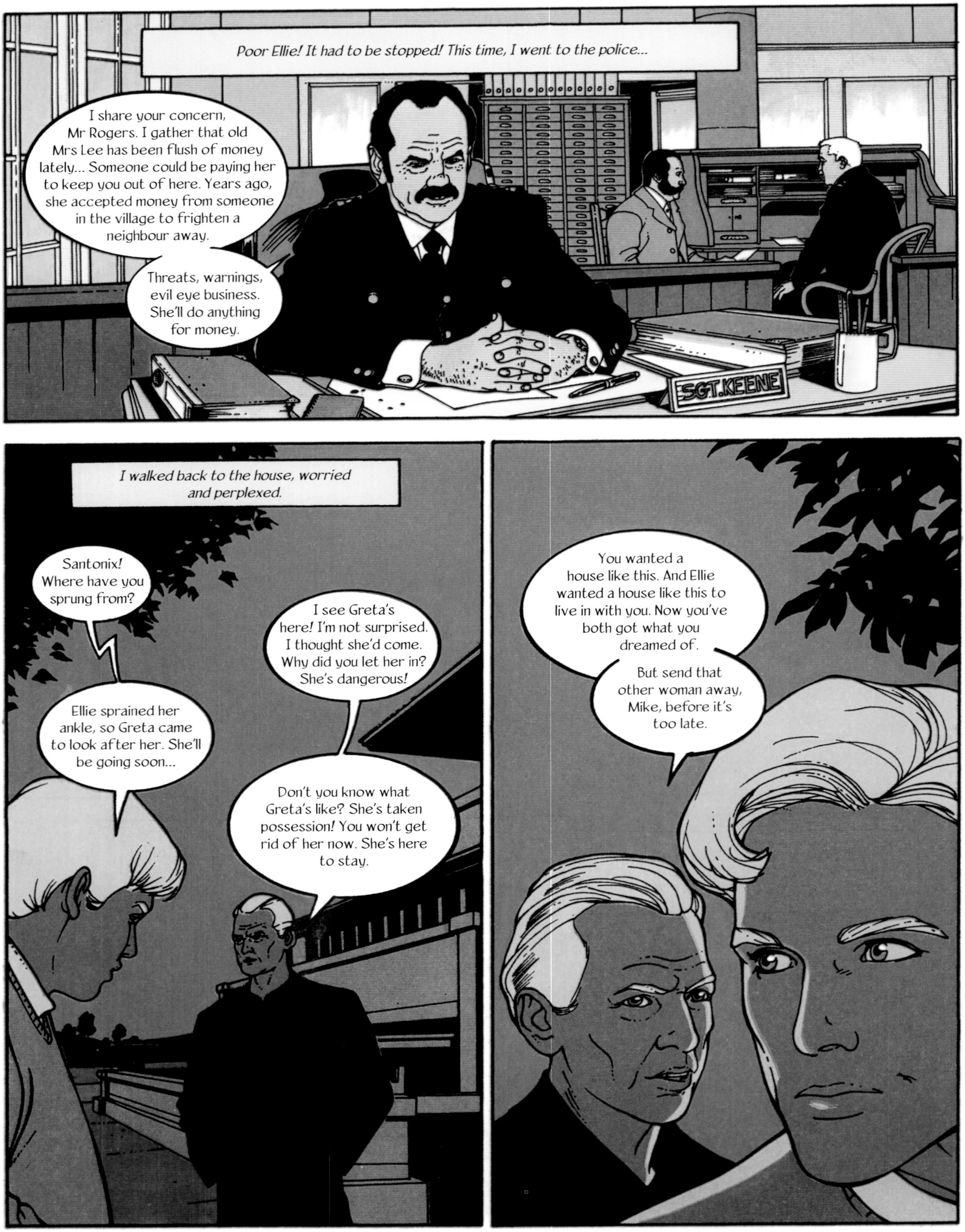
Poor Ellie! It had to be stopped! This time, I went to the police...
I share your concern, Mr Rogers. I gather that old Mrs Lee has been flush of money lately... Someone could be paying her to keep you out of here. Years ago, she accepted money from someone in the village to frighten a neighbour away.
Threats, warnings, evil eye business. She'll do anything for money.
SGT. KEENE
I walked back to the house, worried and perplexed.
Santonix! Where have you sprung from?
Ellie sprained her ankle, so Greta came to look after her. She'll be going soon...
I see Greta's here! I'm not surprised. I thought she'd come. Why did you let her in? She's dangerous!
Don't you know what Greta's like? She's taken possession! You won't get rid of her now. She's here to stay.
You wanted a house like this. And Ellie wanted a house like this to live in with you. Now you've both got what you dreamed of.
But send that other woman away, Mike, before it's too late.

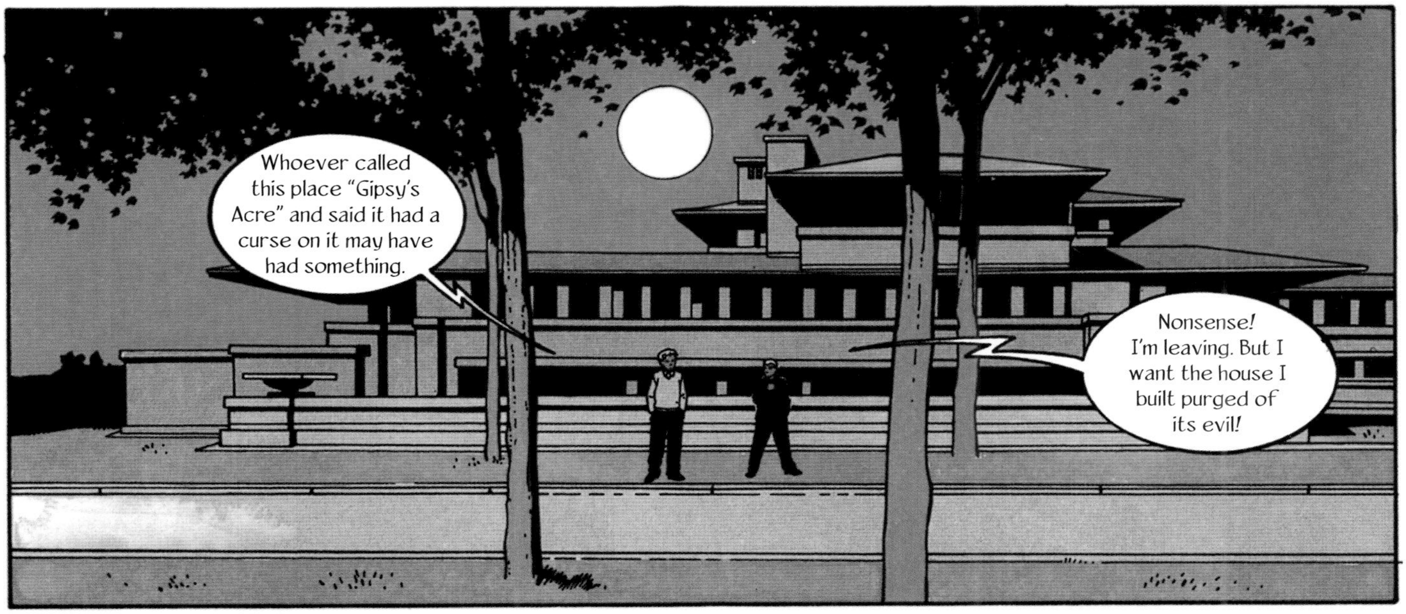
Whoever called this place "Gipsy's Acre" and said it had a curse on it may have had something.
Nonsense! I'm leaving. But I want the house I built purged of its evil!

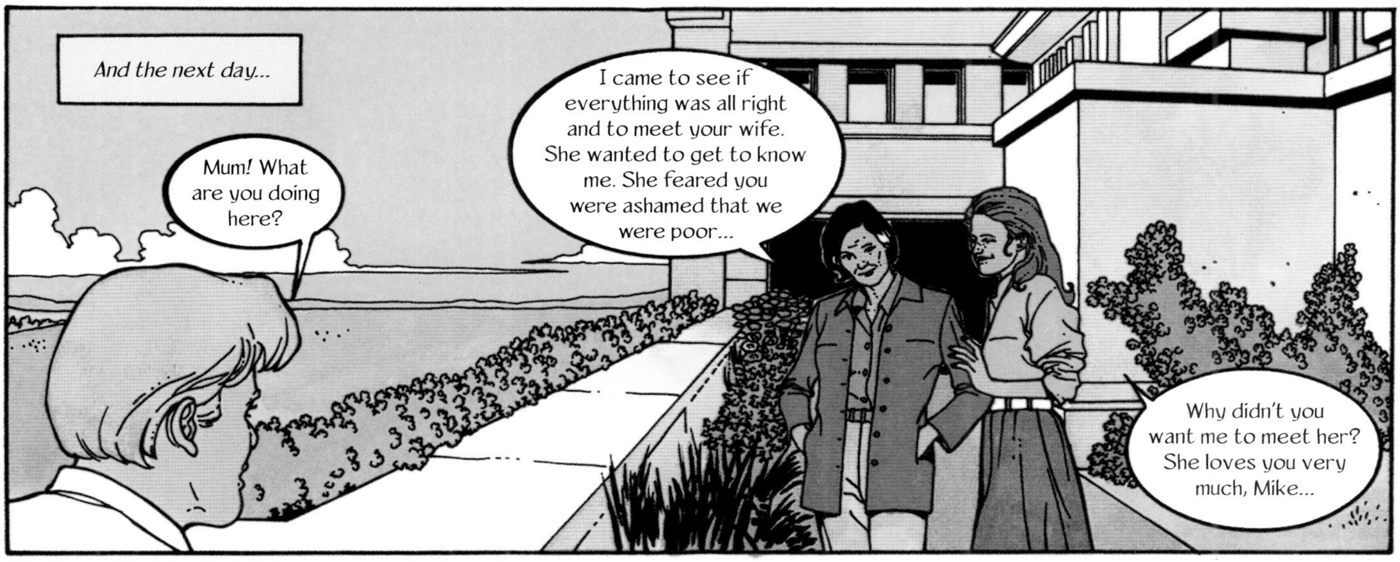
And the next day...
Mum! What are you doing here?
I came to see if everything was all right and to meet your wife. She wanted to get to know me. She feared you were ashamed that we were poor...
Why didn't you want me to meet her? She loves you very much, Mike...

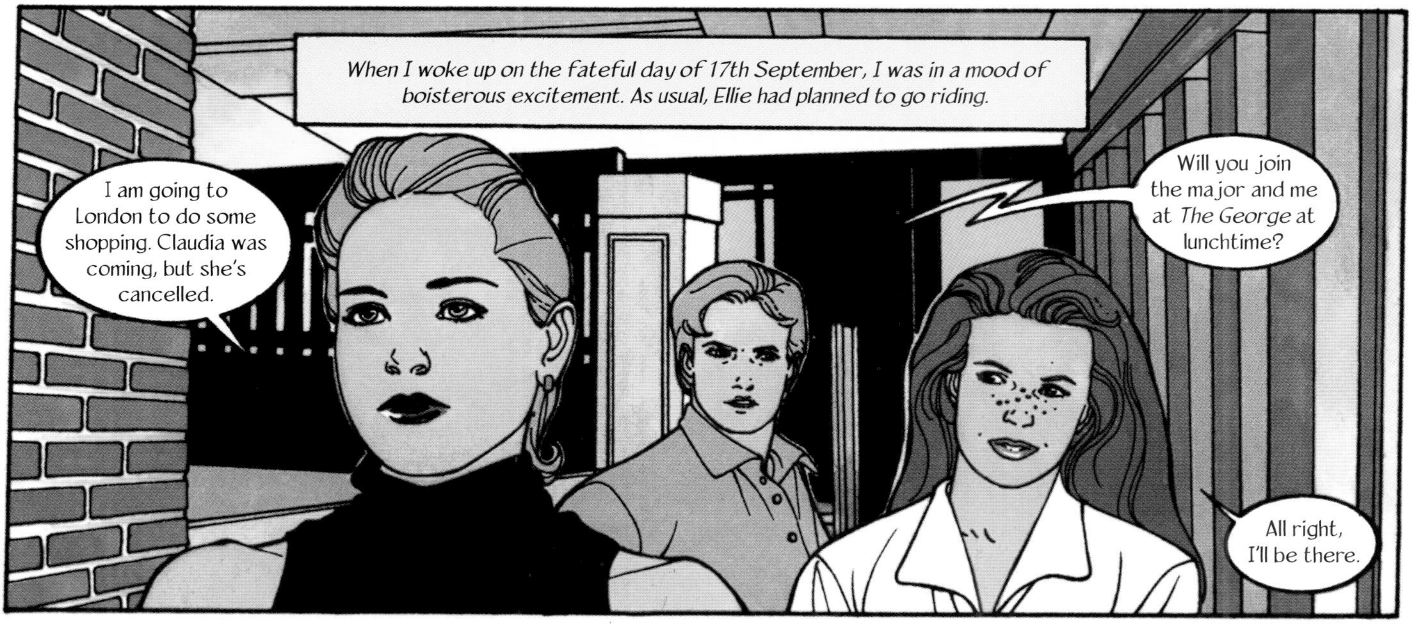
When I woke up on the fateful day of 17th September, I was in a mood of boisterous excitement. As usual, Ellie had planned to go riding.
I am going to London to do some shopping. Claudia was coming, but she's cancelled.
Will you join the major and me at The George at lunchtime?
All right, I'll be there.

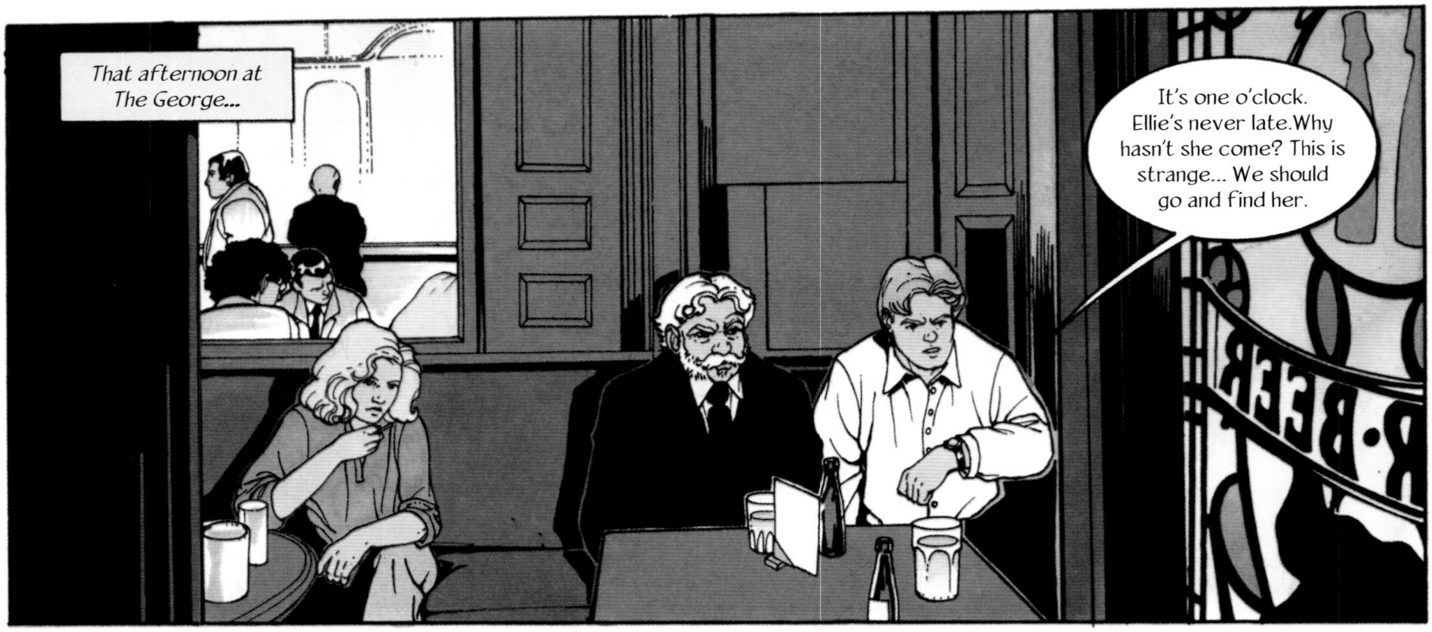
That afternoon at The George...
It's one o'clock. Ellie's never late. Why hasn't she come? This is strange... We should go and find her.

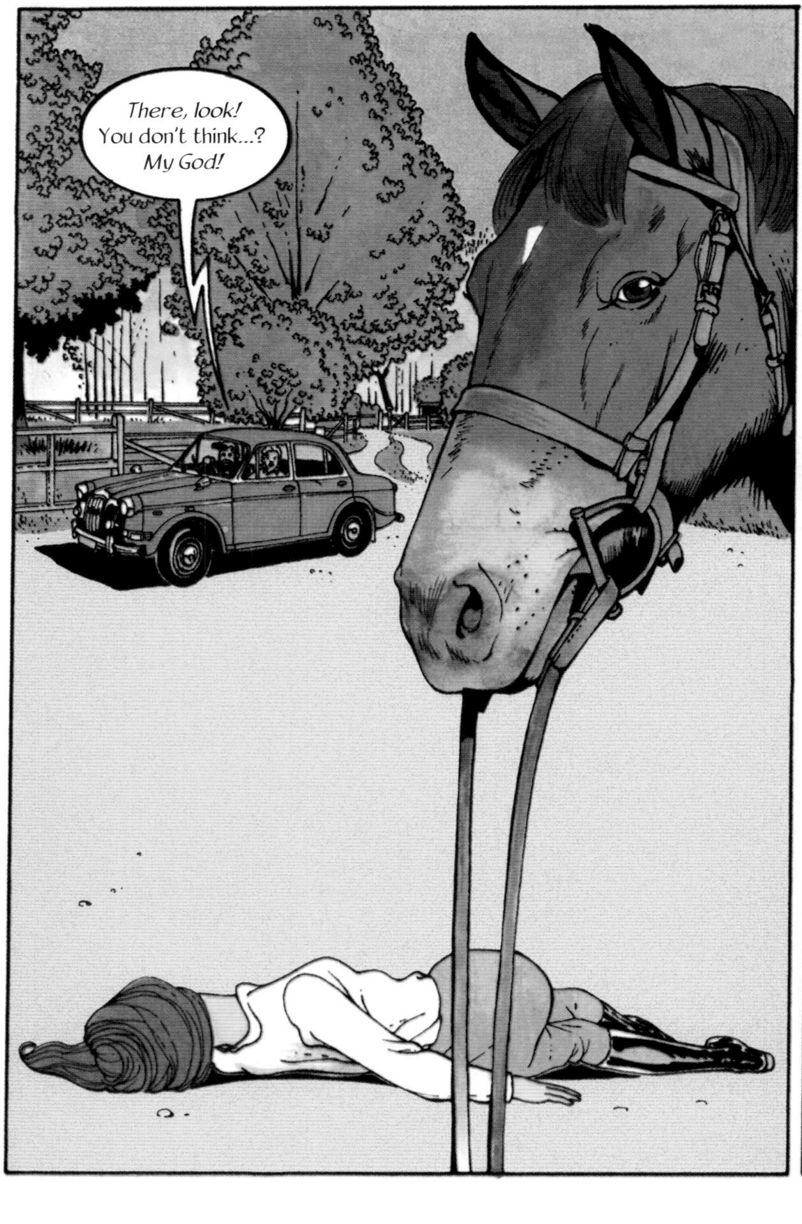
There, look! You don't think...? *My God!*

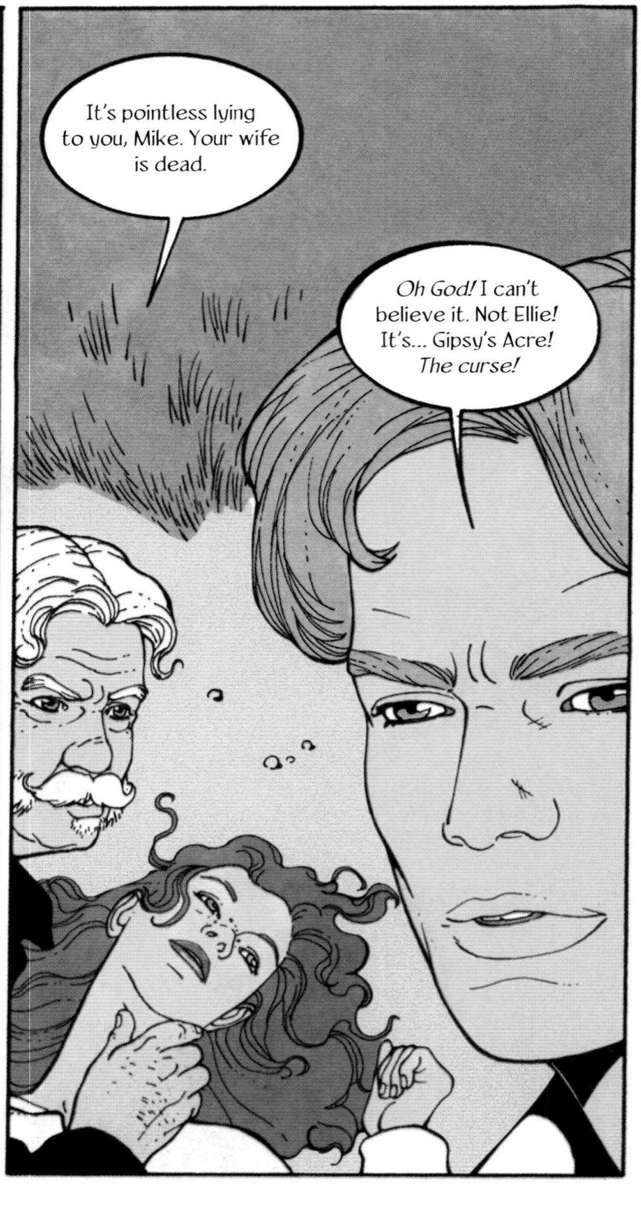
It's pointless lying to you, Mike. Your wife is dead.
Oh God! I can't believe it. Not Ellie! It's... Gipsy's Acre! *The curse!*

The inquest was a revelation. Witnesses claimed to have seen old Mrs Lee not far from the accident, and though she was summoned to the hearing, she had since disappeared. I was determined to get to the bottom of Ellie's death.

I have the feeling that Mrs Lee was out to frighten Ellie right from the beginning. Sergeant Keene told me that she would do anything for money...

But who would have paid Mrs Lee to act in that way? Did Ellie have enemies you didn't know about?

Someone threw a brick through our window this morning, major. It's not the first time. A note on it said, "It was a woman who killed your wife."

Extraordinary! Take this to Sergeant Keene. Perhaps there was a witness of the accident.

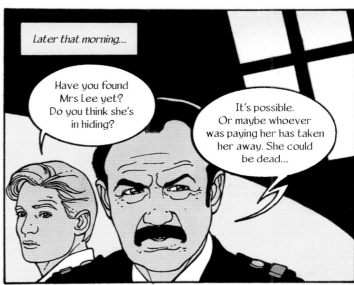

Later that morning...

Have you found Mrs Lee yet? Do you think she's in hiding?

It's possible. Or maybe whoever was paying her has taken her away. She could be dead...

Mr Rogers, do you recognize this lighter? It wouldn't be your wife's, would it? We found it in the Folly close to your house.

No, not with the initial "C"... It could be Cora, her stepmother, or Claudia Hardcastle, her best friend here. But I wouldn't... *oh!*

Now that I think of it... Claudia was married to an American named Lloyd. That's also the name of Ellie's principal trustee!

I left the police station, and by sheer coincidence I passed Claudia Hardcastle outside the post office. It was an awkward moment for both of us...

I'm terribly sorry about Ellie. I hear you are going to America quite soon. If you're thinking of selling your house, I'd rather like to buy if off you.

My brother Rudolf says that this house is the best he's done. I have the means to meet whatever price you ask.

What?!

You told me that you hate modern architecture!

In fact, *Mrs Lloyd*, I have no intention of selling Gipsy's Acre...

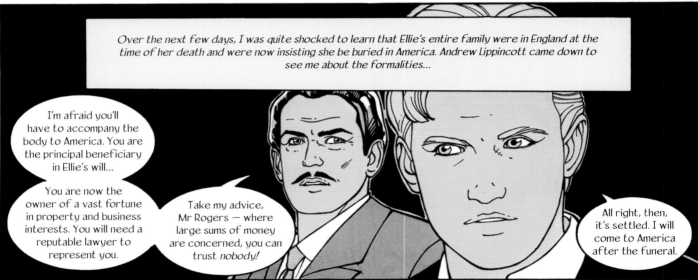

Over the next few days, I was quite shocked to learn that Ellie's entire family were in England at the time of her death and were now insisting she be buried in America. Andrew Lippincott came down to see me about the formalities...

I'm afraid you'll have to accompany the body to America. You are the principal beneficiary in Ellie's will...

You are now the owner of a vast fortune in property and business interests. You will need a reputable lawyer to represent you.

Take my advice, Mr Rogers — where large sums of money are concerned, you can trust *nobody!*

All right, then, it's settled. I will come to America after the funeral.

He's trying to warn me about someone... Cora? Stanford Lloyd? Uncle Frank?

We held a simple funeral service for Ellie in the little church in Market Chadwell. Greta had organized everything...

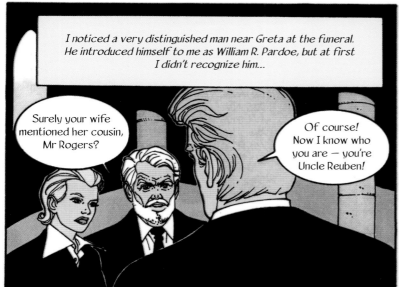

I noticed a very distinguished man near Greta at the funeral. He introduced himself to me as William R. Pardoe, but at first I didn't recognize him...

Surely your wife mentioned her cousin, Mr Rogers?

Of course! Now I know who you are — you're Uncle Reuben!

I don't need to tell you how shocked I was to hear of Ellie's death. I have been England for the past three weeks...

In fact, I saw you in the village pub the morning of... well... the accident.

I was indeed there, in the company of Major Phillpot. Ellie didn't mention that you were in England...

I hadn't told her. I came with Cora Van Stuyvesant, who wanted some advice on a house she's thinking of buying here. She was staying here with a friend — Claudia Hardcastle. She knew her from America.

So that's why Claudia couldn't come with me to London that day...

After all the confusion, I was happy to leave Greta in charge of the house and fly with Ellie's body to New York. Greta warned me that I was venturing into a kind of jungle...

37

I met the lawyer that Lippincott had recommended. He warned me that the family had already tried to get their hands on certain assets. Four days later, as I was leaving for Ellie's burial at her family's tomb, I received a startling letter from Major Phillpot...

My head was reeling! Mrs Lee's body had been found in the disused quarry near Gipsy's Acre. But even more surprising, the major also wrote that Claudia Hardcastle had been taken ill and died. As I stood in the cemetary, I knew I didn't belong here — I had to go home!

On the eve of my departure, I had a long conversation with Mr Lippincott...

Where do you think you will live now, Mr Rogers? In view of recent events, I suppose you'll be selling...

...Gipsy's Acre? Never! Greta Andersen has been taking care of the place. I am grateful to her for all that she has done for me since Ellie's death. I don't know what I'd have done without her.

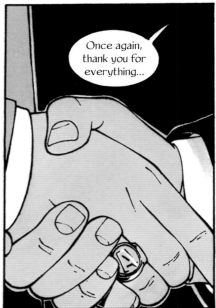

Once again, thank you for everything...

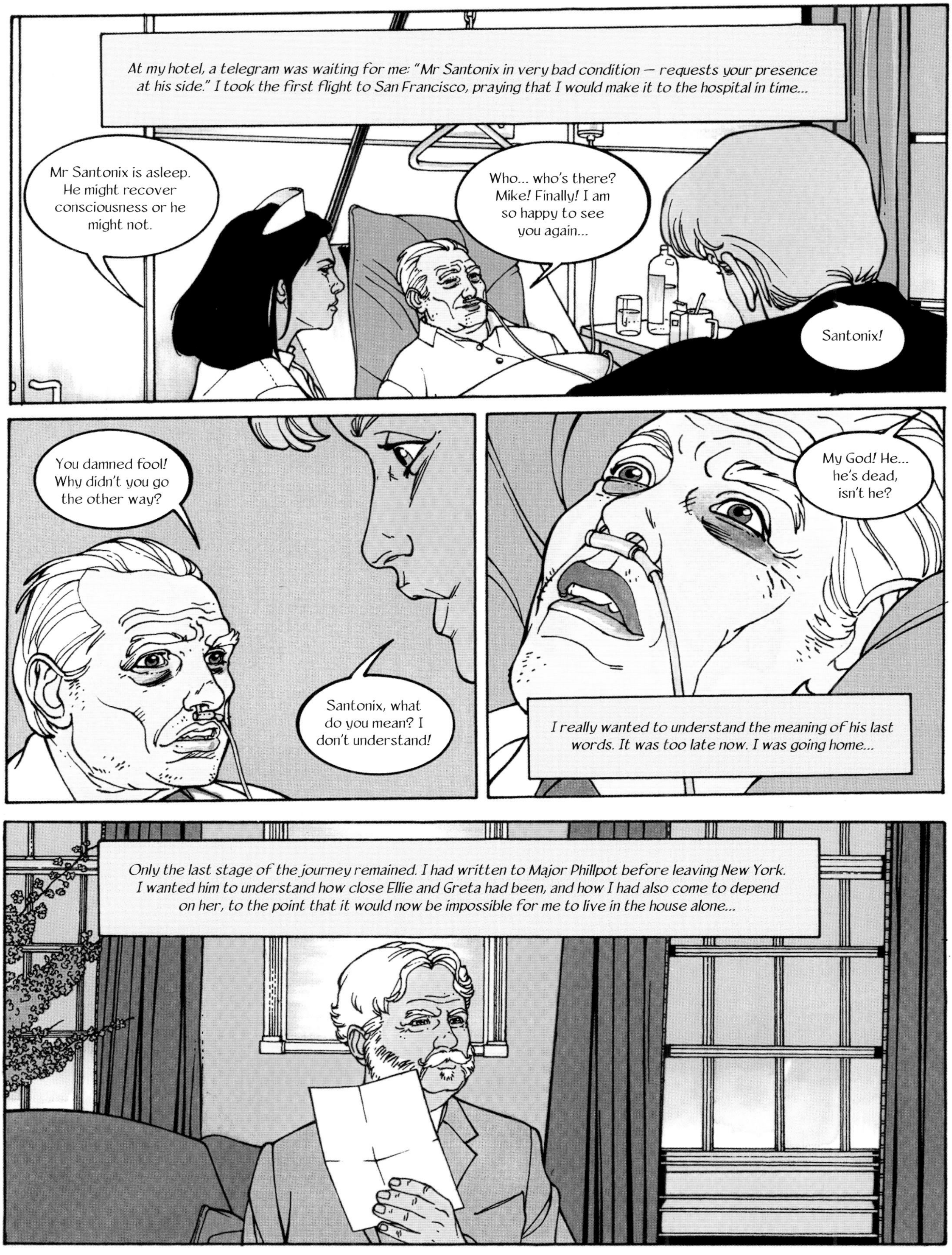
At my hotel, a telegram was waiting for me: "Mr Santonix in very bad condition — requests your presence at his side." I took the first flight to San Francisco, praying that I would make it to the hospital in time...
Mr Santonix is asleep. He might recover consciousness or he might not.
Who... who's there? Mike! Finally! I am so happy to see you again...
Santonix!
You damned fool! Why didn't you go the other way?
Santonix, what do you mean? I don't understand!
My God! He... he's dead, isn't he?
I really wanted to understand the meaning of his last words. It was too late now. I was going home...
Only the last stage of the journey remained. I had written to Major Phillpot before leaving New York. I wanted him to understand how close Ellie and Greta had been, and how I had also come to depend on her, to the point that it would now be impossible for me to live in the house alone...

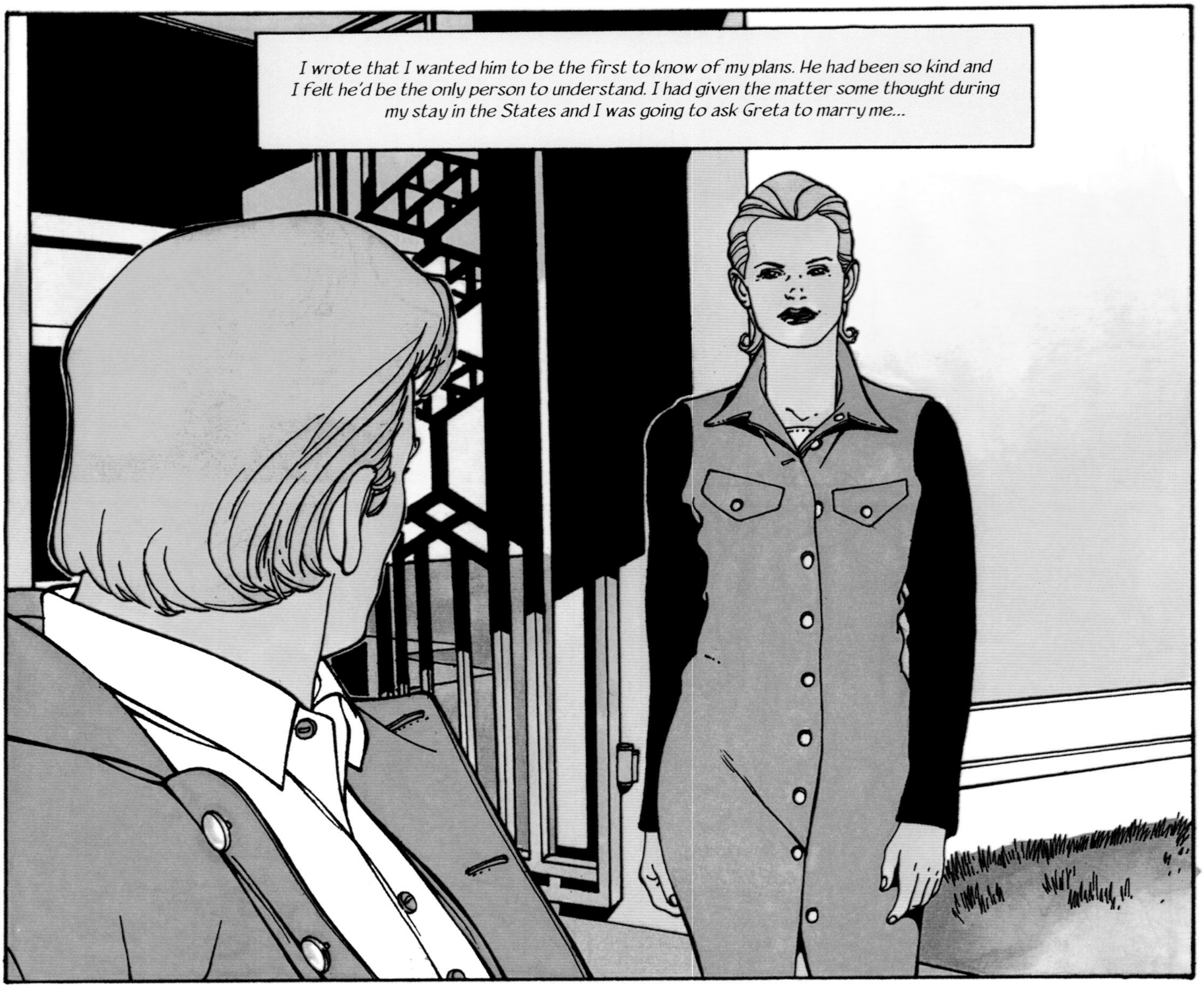
I wrote that I wanted him to be the first to know of my plans. He had been so kind and I felt he'd be the only person to understand. I had given the matter some thought during my stay in the States and I was going to ask Greta to marry me...

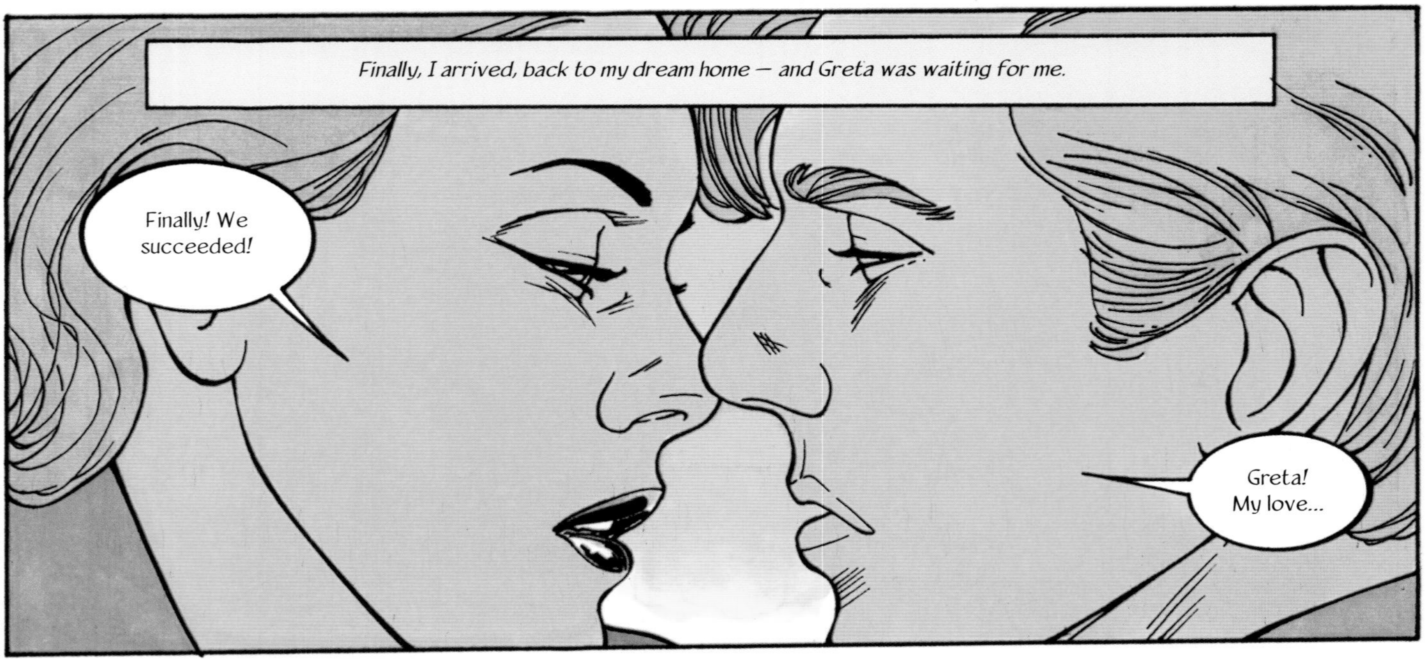
Finally, I arrived, back to my dream home — and Greta was waiting for me.
Finally! We succeeded!
Greta! My love...

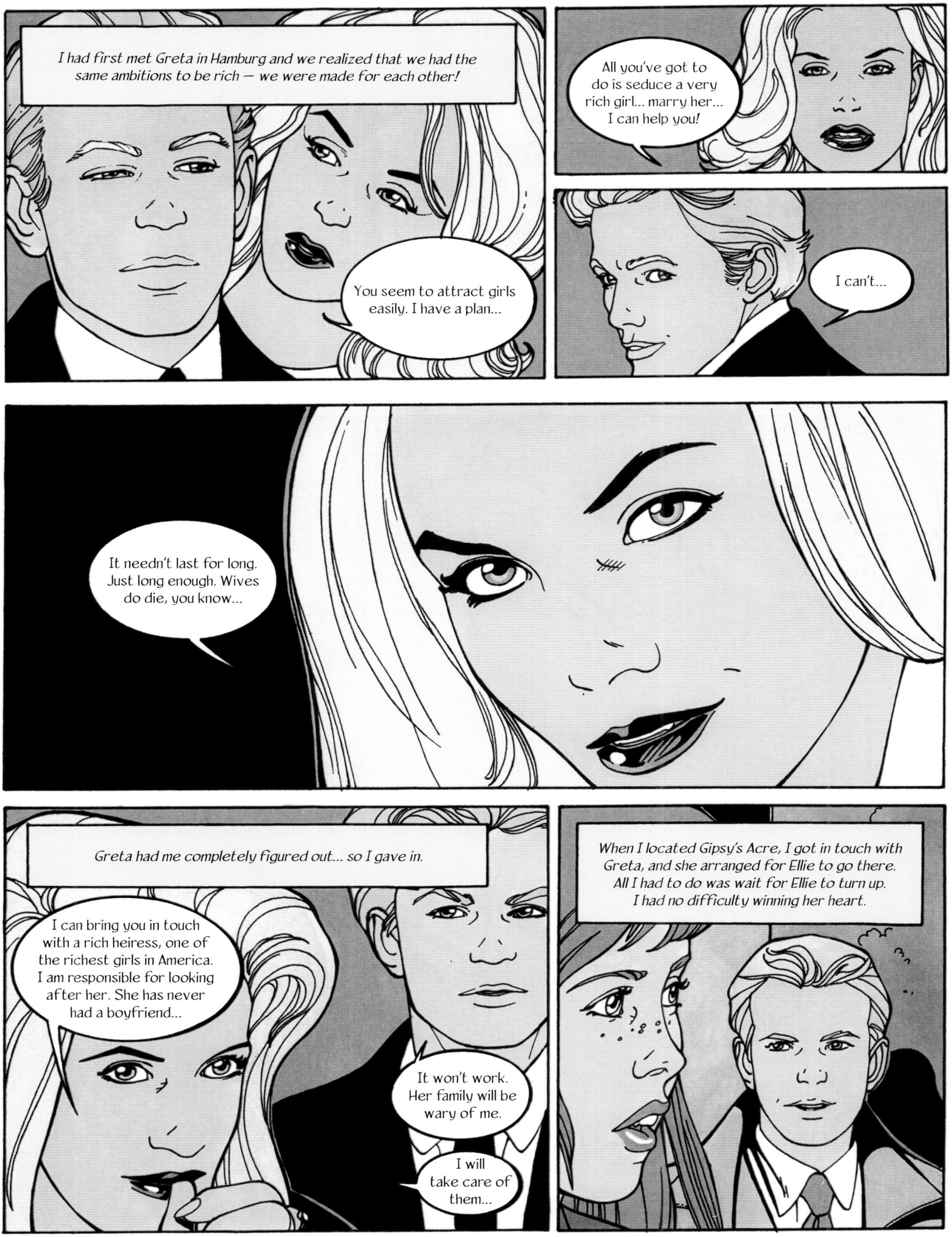
I had first met Greta in Hamburg and we realized that we had the same ambitions to be rich — we were made for each other!
You seem to attract girls easily. I have a plan...
All you've got to do is seduce a very rich girl... marry her... I can help you!
I can't...
It needn't last for long. Just long enough. Wives do die, you know...
Greta had me completely figured out... so I gave in.
I can bring you in touch with a rich heiress, one of the richest girls in America. I am responsible for looking after her. She has never had a boyfriend...
It won't work. Her family will be wary of me.
I will take care of them...
When I located Gipsy's Acre, I got in touch with Greta, and she arranged for Ellie to go there. All I had to do was wait for Ellie to turn up. I had no difficulty winning her heart.

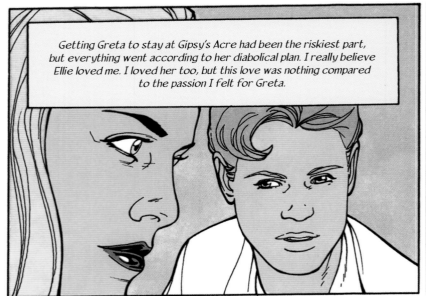

Getting Greta to stay at Gipsy's Acre had been the riskiest part, but everything went according to her diabolical plan. I really believe Ellie loved me. I loved her too, but this love was nothing compared to the passion I felt for Greta.

Well, let's celebrate our victory!

Excellent idea, my darling!

I haven't told you yet, Santonix died a few days back. I was there. He said something to me... that I was a damned fool and should have gone the other way. I think he had figured it out.

Forget him, like we must forget Ellie... Let's drink!

A little while later...

Mike, you're shivering. What's wrong?

It's impossible! *Look!* There — in the garden... it's *Ellie!* ELLIE!!!

Don't be ridiculous — you are imagining things. Pull yourself together!

It *was* Ellie. She was standing there — looking at me. But she couldn't see me!

It's as if I wasn't there any more. Ellie was born to *Sweet Delight* — but I was born to *Endless Night*...

Ellie should have lived instead of you! I am sure now that I loved her!

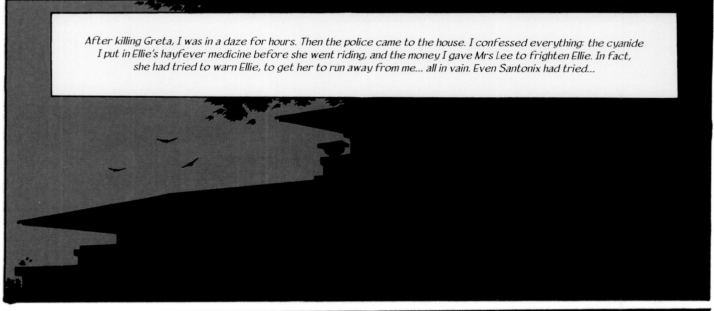

After killing Greta, I was in a daze for hours. Then the police came to the house. I confessed everything: the cyanide I put in Ellie's hayfever medicine before she went riding, and the money I gave Mrs Lee to frighten Ellie. In fact, she had tried to warn Ellie, to get her to run away from me... all in vain. Even Santonix had tried...

It was Claudia's accidental death after taking Ellie's pills that set the police on to me. They found traces of the poison on her lighter.

43

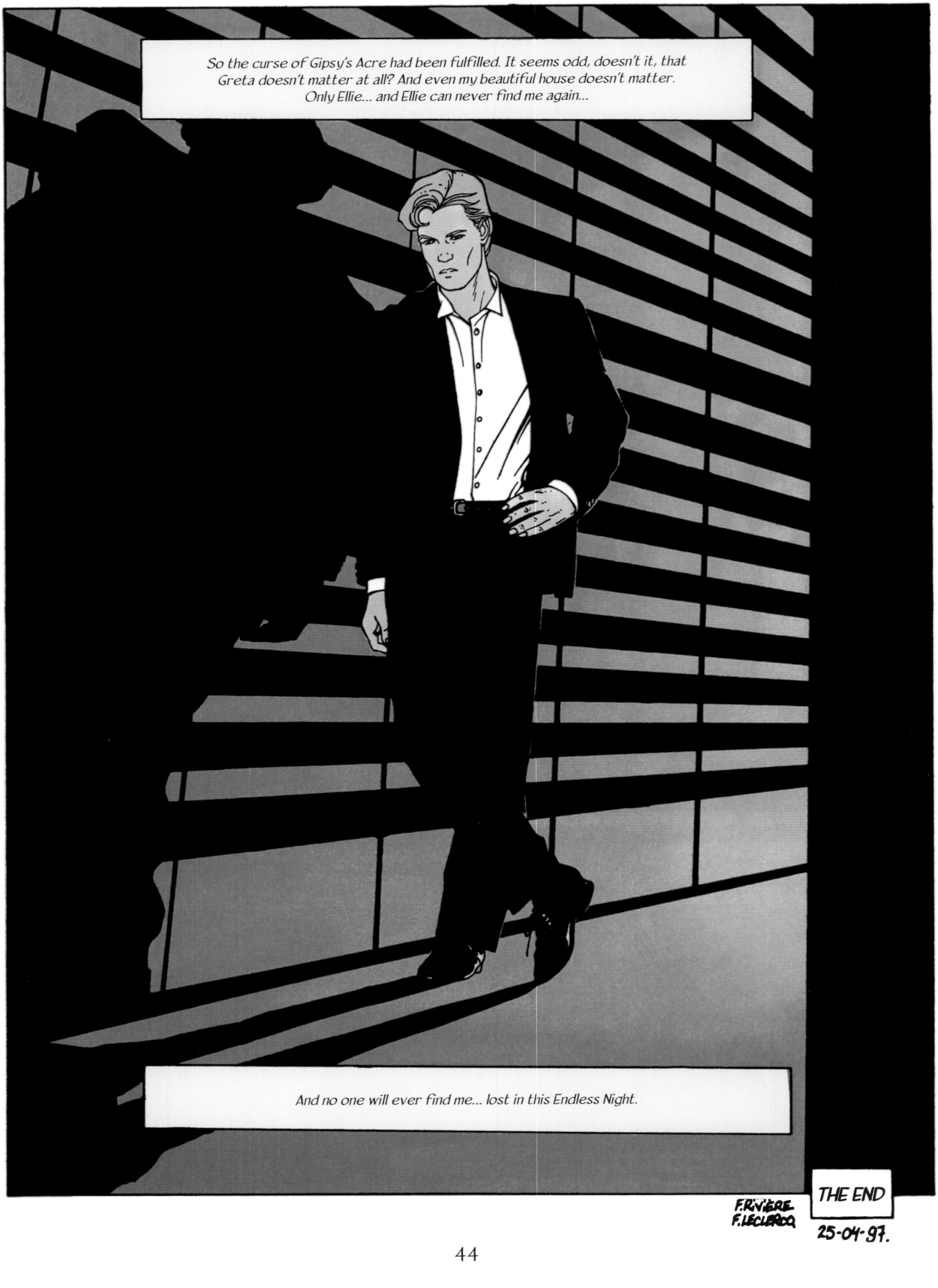
So the curse of Gipsy's Acre had been fulfilled. It seems odd, doesn't it, that Greta doesn't matter at all? And even my beautiful house doesn't matter. Only Ellie... and Ellie can never find me again...
And no one will ever find me... lost in this Endless Night.
THE END
F.RIVIERE
F.LECLERCQ
25-04-97.

AGATHA CHRISTIE (1890—1976) is known throughout the world as *The Queen of Crime*. Her first book, *The Mysterious Affair at Styles*, was written during the First World War and introduced us to Hercule Poirot, the Belgian detective with the "Little Grey Cells", who was destined to reappear in nearly 100 different adventures over the next 50 years. Agatha also created the elderly crime-solver, Miss Marple, as well as more than 2,000 colourful characters across her 80 crime novels and short story collections. Agatha Christie's books have sold over one billion copies in the English language and another billion in more than 100 countries, making her the best-selling novelist in history. Now, following years of successful adaptations including stage, films, television, radio, audiobooks and interactive games, some of her most famous novels, including *Murder on the Orient Express*, *The Secret Adversary* and *The Murder at the Vicarage*, have been adapted into comic strips so that they may be enjoyed by yet another generation of readers.

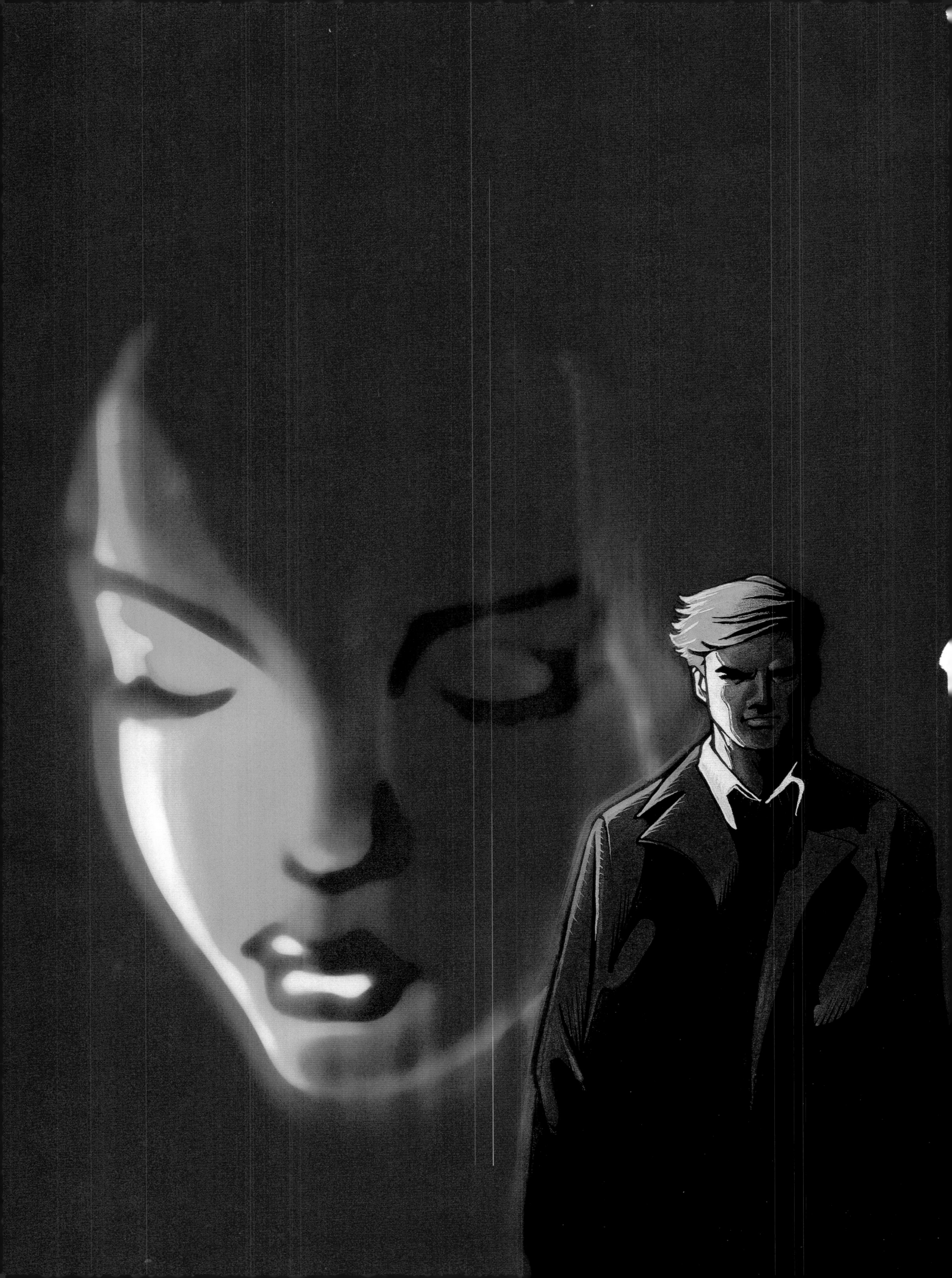